She slid her foot back to step away. His hand shot out and latched on to her waist. Dante closed the scant distance between them and pressed his solid body against hers.

"Don't stand so close if you don't want to get caught."

Desire coated every nuance of his voice. The air around them shifted, crackling and sparking with the anger, annoyance and attraction simmering between them. The line between anger and desire was thin, and when his long fingers flexed against her waist, the line snapped. He infuriated her. The audacity of him paying for the meal, declaring himself competition, insisting that being zapped by the electric current between them was inevitable. Yet she couldn't listen to the faint voice in her mind that said to pull away. Sucking in a breath, she didn't smell cologne; instead, the clean smell of masculine soap and the intoxicating heat of his body made her mouth water.

"Now that I've got you," he said, his tenor lowering to a seductive bass, "what are you going to do?"

Dear Reader,

If you have young kids you probably spend a lot of your television time watching cartoons and kids' shows (it can't be just me). Little did I know that a guest appearance by a group called Nuttin' But Stringz on my kid's favorite show would not only inspire me to create a Pandora station, but later a book. Dante Wilson is the hero in *A Malibu Kind of Romance* and an R & B superstar. He's been in the music industry since he was thirteen, and now he wants to try something new. I knew immediately the music he wanted to play would be similar to the music of Nuttin' But Stringz, who play a blend of classical, hip-hop, jazz and R & B.

While you're reading *A Malibu Kind of Romance*, if you have a hard time "hearing" the music, check out the group. Maybe you'll get a little inspiration, too.

Synithia

A MALIBU KIND OF Romance

SYNITHIA WILLIAMS

HARLEQUIN® KIMANI™ ROMANCE

Recycling programs
for this product may
not exist in your area.

ISBN-13: 978-0-373-86464-5

A Malibu Kind of Romance

Copyright © 2016 by Synithia R. Williams

HARLEQUIN®
www.Harlequin.com

Printed in U.S.A.

Synithia Williams has been an avid romance novel lover since picking up her first at the age of thirteen. It was only natural that she would begin penning her own romances soon after—much to the chagrin of her high school math teachers. She's a native of South Carolina and now writes romances as hot as their southern settings. Outside of writing, she works on water quality and sustainability issues for local government. She's married to her own personal hero, and they have two sons, who've convinced her that professional wrestling and superheroes are supreme entertainment. When she isn't working, writing or being a wife and mother, she's usually bingeing on TV series, playing around on social media or planning her next girls' night out with friends. You can learn more about Synithia by visiting her website, www.synithiawilliams.com, where she blogs about writing, life and relationships.

Books by Synithia Williams

Harlequin Kimani Romance

A New York Kind of Love
A Malibu Kind of Romance

Visit the Author Profile page at
Harlequin.com for more titles.

To my parents, Lisa and Sam,
thank you for always supporting my dreams.

Chapter 1

Dante Wilson stared at the supermodel twins dancing together at his post-concert party in Vegas and had one thought: he loved his life! What wasn't there to love? He was one of the world's bestselling artists, his family ran a music dynasty, he'd finished a sold-out world tour and he was pretty sure he'd be going home with one or both of the twins. He leaned back against the plush leather sofa, took a sip of the champagne in his hand and grinned.

The Vegas strip was a colorful backdrop outside the window of the penthouse suite, which was filled with celebrities, their entourages and musicians—all there to help him celebrate. The guy to Dante's right, basketball star Jacobe Jenkins, pulled his long designer-jean-clad legs in and leaned forward, resting his elbows on his knees. "I know what you're thinking."

Dante shifted in his seat. He'd lost his dress shirt earlier while dancing, and wore only a white T-shirt and black slacks. "If you're assuming my thoughts have something to do with the twins, then you're right."

Jacobe chuckled. "I should have bet money on that. You go through more women than any other guy I know. And I'm surrounded by professional basketball players all day."

"Perks of the job," Dante said. "But after tonight I'm slowing down with the female distractions. Tonight's about releasing some steam after the tour before getting back into the studio. Though I love partying, I'm going to have to do less of this for a while." He waved his hand to indicate the energetic crowd.

"Damn, Dante," Jacobe said, once again stretching out his legs. "You just got back in the country, and you're going back to the studio."

"To stay on top of my game, I can never really take a break. Plus, I'm excited to get back to Malibu and get to work on the music I want to do."

Jacobe raised a brow. "That classical stuff?"

Dante shook his head. "It's not classical stuff. It's a fusion of hip-hop, jazz and rock *with* classical influence. Wait until you hear it—you'll dig it."

Jacobe gave Dante a skeptical look before he turned to watch one of the many beauties at the party walking by. Jacobe's skepticism didn't deter Dante's confidence in his next move. Not much anyway. Dante had built a solid career using the Wilson family legacy and his own talent. He could sing, play several different instruments and dance. After seventeen years doing the music his family and their label wanted him to do, Dante was ready to do his own thing.

Not that he regretted seventeen years of pop stardom. Show business was in his family's blood—starting with his great-grandfather, who'd performed on the Chitlin' Circuit in the 1950s, to his grandfather, who'd started his own record label in the 1970s. Then to Dante's father, who with a smooth baritone singing voice, hit songs and a shrewd business sense, turned that label into one of the country's most successful. The biggest names in music signed with W. M. Records.

Dante was fiercely proud of his family's legacy. But pride didn't diminish a growing frustration with the pressure to keep doing the same type of music that everyone else was doing.

"Are you sure the music you're doing will be successful?" Jacobe asked.

Dante shrugged. "I can't say one hundred percent, but I know there's an audience. The group I'm working with, Strings A Flame, they've got a following. If I sign them to W. M. Records and record an album with them, then that's all it'll take."

"You're pretty confident in your pull," Jacobe said, turning away from the woman he'd been watching.

"I've been around for nearly twenty years. I'm allowed to be confident in my staying power. I know the market isn't as big—that's why I'm opening a nightclub. I'll debut the music there, see how the fans react, then go from there."

"You've got it all planned out."

"Always," he said with a confidence that he couldn't allow to waiver. The only hitch in his perfect plan was his dad. Otis Wilson wanted hip-hop and R&B right now, the more commercial the better. He'd originally brushed off Dante's plans to sign S.A.F. and hadn't shown any interest in backing an album. He needed the nightclub to be successful to convince his dad otherwise.

Jacobe looked at Dante. "What do you know about opening a nightclub?"

"Nothing. I'm partnering with Raymond, but we may still need someone to come in and handle the day-to-day." Dante pointed to Raymond, who was walking over to where he and Jacobe were sitting.

Raymond was an up-and-coming star in the R&B world with two hit albums in the past five years. He had enough popularity to make some people think Raymond's future in the Rock and Roll Hall of Fame was set, but Dante had seen enough artists crash and burn to know two hit albums didn't mean a thing. However, the kid was smart and had invested his money in other ventures outside the entertainment industry, including a nightclub called Masquerade in Atlanta that he and another rapper opened a few years ago. It was now the hottest spot in the city. When Raymond mentioned opening a place on the West Coast, Dante immediately brought up his idea. Raymond had agreed after listening to some of the music Dante and S.A.F. had put together.

"Dante," Raymond said with a grin on his face. He held out his hand and gave Dante a fist bump before doing the same with Jacobe.

"This party is where it's at," Raymond said.

"I told you the best way to celebrate the end of a tour is with a party in Vegas," Dante said as he and Raymond slapped hands again.

The song changed, and the same twin models who'd had Dante's attention before gyrated to the music.

Dante sipped the champagne in his hand and grinned at the women, who both blew kisses his way.

"Most definitely the way to end a tour," Raymond said, grinning. "Did you tell Jacobe about our plans for the club?"

"I was just telling him about that."

Raymond nodded and grinned. "It's going to be hot, right?"

Jacobe lifted his chin in agreement. "Nothing Dante has done thus far has failed. I don't see why this would. Even though I'm still trying to imagine the music. I keep imagining symphonies with rapping when I think about it."

"I'll send you one of our songs. That'll help," Dante said, still not bothered. Jacobe was a die-hard classic hip-hop fan, and he had a hard time with any other variation in the genre.

Dante looked at Raymond. "It wouldn't hurt to find another partner to come in and help oversee the details of the development," he said. "W. M. Records has a firm it's used for the other nightclubs the label has invested in, but I don't want to use them. They'll go to my dad for his influence, and he'll turn the place into another carbon copy of an LA club. That's not what I'm going for."

Raymond snapped his finger. "I've got someone in mind."

"Really? Who?"

"You ever heard of Julie Dominick?"

Dante ran through the females he may have heard about but came up empty. "Should I know her?"

"She's the woman that handled the development of Masquerade."

Dante's brows rose. "Really?"

"That's my girl, Julie. She negotiated the deal to land that prime location in Buckhead and kept other investors from snagging it up. She oversaw the entire operation, from acquisition to construction, and did a damn good job."

Jacobe chuckled. "What, is she paying you to be her public relations person?"

Raymond shook his head. "Nah, I just wanted you to know the type of work she can do. We should consider her."

"Working her magic in Atlanta isn't the same as working her magic in California," Dante said. "I'd rather go with someone who knows the ins and outs on this side of the country."

"I know Julie—she can do it." Confidence and affection filled Raymond's voice.

Dante's eyes narrowed. "How do you know her? This isn't some old girlfriend you're trying to give the hookup to?"

"Nah, not like that. Julie and I are cool. We met in college, and she's been my homegirl ever since. She got me started in music actually, promoting my music and getting me gigs in and around Atlanta. Now she's started her own development firm, and I want to help her out."

"Is that all? No guy I know just helps out a female for no reason."

Raymond rubbed his jaw and lifted a shoulder. "I wouldn't mind if Julie and I became more than friends one day."

"I figured."

"But it's not like that. Julie is the kind of woman

you make your number one chick. We've talked about finally getting together if both of us were single when we turned thirty. That's only a few years away. Who knows—this may bring us together."

A sexy woman in a skimpy red dress walked past. Raymond and Jacobe both went slack jawed and watched her walk by with more than a little interest. Raymond, ever bold, reached out and took her hand, then pulled her against his side. The woman giggled, wrapping her arms around Raymond's neck.

Dante chuckled and shook his head. "You're ready to settle down, huh?"

Raymond wiggled his brows. "I said a few years off. Come on—look up Julie. She's opened some other spots on the East Coast. We can at least meet with her and then decide."

Dante's cell phone vibrated in his pocket. He pulled it out to find a picture of his father, in his best blue pinstripe suit sitting behind his desk at W. M. Records, on the screen. "I'll think about meeting her. Excuse me, fellas." He stood and punched the button to answer the call.

Dante put the phone to his ear. "Dad, hold on a minute."

He walked away from the main area of the party and into the suite's master bedroom, which was, thankfully, empty. "You still there?"

"Sounds like one hell of a party." Otis Wilson's deep baritone, which was the hallmark of his career, came through the phone.

"You know I like to celebrate the end of a tour in style."

Otis laughed. "I don't blame you. Man, if you could have seen the parties we had back in the day."

"I heard the stories. You guys partied too hard for me."

"That's the truth," Otis said, his voice laced with nostalgia. "What are you doing after you leave Vegas?"

Dante fought not to sigh. He'd told his dad during the entire concert tour what he planned to do. "I'm going to Malibu to look into opening my club."

"You're still on that? Come on, Dante—why are you wasting your time?"

"It's not wasting time. I've spent seventeen years doing what the market told me to do. Now I want to pursue my own things."

"Dante, you can dabble in that classical–hip-hop fusion mess on the side, but the money is in mainstream music. I just left a meeting with Antwan, and he's interested in doing a joint album with you." Antwan was the biggest name in hip-hop, and the fact that he was unhappy with his label was no secret. Ever since that news had gone public, Otis had let Dante know he would try to recruit Antwan to W. M. Records. Hard.

"Having Raymond on your concert tour gave you a boost with the younger generation. If you do an album with Antwan, then follow it with your own R&B, you'll sell even more."

The same song Otis had sung since Dante announced his tour. Otis always followed the money, which normally meant following the mainstream trends.

"I've sold enough that I trust being able to try something new. I'll consider a collaboration with Antwan after the club is up and going."

"You put out that crappy music and your name will

be nothing. We can't afford the hit. Not after what your sister pulled last year."

Dante pinched the bridge of his nose. His sister had a strong pop music career, but, for some reason, she'd tried to go hard-core hip-hop the previous year. The only thing hard about her album was how hard it hit the bottom of the charts.

"What Star tried and what I'm trying are not the same."

"Dante, I need you to do the album with Antwan." The urgency of Otis's tone was unexpected.

Dante frowned. "What's going on?"

"The thing with your sister was just the icing on the cake. We've got artists that are considering not resigning, and sales are down. We need Antwan to breathe new life into W. M. Records and another set of hit albums to rebuild confidence with our current artists."

"How bad are sales?"

"I didn't want to get into this, but we've gone down about five percent the past two years. I wouldn't worry, we've had down years before, but if we lose some artists and can't sign a big name, then we may be talking double-digit losses. They haven't crucified us in the business news yet. But another year with profit losses, and they will."

"Damn," Dante grunted and ran a hand over his forehead. He sat back on the bed while his dad's revelation took root in his brain. The Wilson legacy, and the success of W. M. Records, was what he'd lived for and built his career on. If they had multiple years of losses, even small ones, pretty soon the speculators would begin to spread rumors that things weren't going well at W. M. Records. Artists would jump ship. Sales would dwindle. Best case, they'd take several years to rebuild. Worst case, they would fold or have to consider a merger with another label just to stay afloat.

"Go ahead and open the club," Otis said. "You mentioned that Raymond wants to put his name on it. Fine, that'll help. But before you turn it into some hippie hangout, think about doing the album with Antwan, and maybe booking some of our commercial artists there instead."

Dante hated the idea of his dream becoming something else, but he also hated the idea of his family's legacy suffering. "I'll think about it."

"Good."

They talked for a few more minutes. Afterward, Dante tossed his phone on the bed. The fate of W. M. Records and the good argument Otis had for Dante to continue making the music that sold swirled in his brain. He'd never considered that what happened to Star could happen to him, but with the state of affairs at W. M. Records, it was a real concern. As much as he wanted to try his hand at new, different music, he honestly loved his lifestyle and the perks of being famous. One bad album wouldn't ruin him, but it could take him from being one of the most celebrated men in the music industry to a laughingstock.

Dante swore and rubbed his temples. *Damn.* He really didn't want to think about that.

There was a knock on the door before it opened. The two models he'd watched dance before peaked their heads in. Their grins promised a welcome distraction from his shaky confidence—something he'd never felt before. Smiling, Dante waved the women in. Tomorrow he'd worry about what to do with his music career. Tonight his music was still popular and so was he. Time to get back to relaxing after another success-ful tour and worry about reality later.

Chapter 2

Julie Dominick hung up the phone on her desk and jumped up from the leather chair. Her red high heels tapped on the tile floor as she rushed across the hall to the office of her business partner, Evette Dean. She gave two swift knocks on Evette's open door before hurrying in.

"You'll never guess who I just talked to," Julie said in a rush.

Evette slowly turned away from her wide-screen monitor and raised a brow—her natural response whenever Julie came to her bouncing in excitement. Evette's light brown hair was twisted in the usual no-nonsense bun at the back of her head, and her polka-dot tan blouse and matching black pencil skirt were flawless, as always. If not for the spark in Evette's dark eyes, Julie would think she hadn't garnered her friend's interest.

"Then you better tell me."

Julie stood before Evette's neatly arranged desk. "Raymond just called."

Evette's raised brows lowered into a frown. The spark of interest was gone. She waved a hand and turned back to her monitor. "I thought you were talking about someone."

Julie reached over and placed a hand over Evette's hands, which were already typing away on the keyboard. "You will never guess what he wanted."

Evette sighed and turned back to Julie. "What did he want?"

"He's opening a nightclub, and he wants us to manage the development."

The interest returned full force. Evette sat forward, her eyes wide. "Are you serious?"

"There are two things I don't play around with, and that's business and money."

"That's great! When, where, what type of club?"

Julie waved her hands back and forth to stop the flow of questions. "He's finished the concert tour, and now he's in Malibu, California. He wants someplace upscale but with a casual vibe where they can host live performances. He's already bought the location and needs another partner to help oversee the day-to-day operations."

"When are you going?" Evette's voice indicated that Julie should be packing instead of talking.

Julie took a deep breath and fell into the leather chair across from Evette's glass-top desk. "I'm not sure if I'm going."

Evette's excitement morphed into confusion. Not surprising. Out of the two of them, Julie was definitely the one who didn't hesitate when the time came to make bold decisions. "You're not sure?" Evette asked. "When have you ever not been sure about doing something this big?"

More times than Julie would ever admit. Faking confidence after walking away from Nexon-Jones, a powerhouse in the nightclub and restaurant development world, to start her own firm was proof of that.

Some thought she was crazy for leaving Nexon-Jones, where she was on the fast track to being one of their most promising agents. The decision had been easy after her boss had asked her to get a little more *comfortable* with a potential client. Julie walked and started Dominant Development. A bold name for a bold move. Go hard or go home.

The bold move worked enough to get Evette to walk away with her, and their combined determination had led to Dominant Development's name being behind the openings of nightclubs around the southeast with more than a few celebrities tied to them. Having one of R&B's newest stars as a best friend didn't hurt either. Raymond had helped her get her first nightclub opened at the start of his career and later had introduced her to his celebrity friends. This was the first time he'd brought up opening a new place with her.

"We need to fix the situation in Miami," Julie said.

"All the more reason to go," Evette countered. "If you do this, everyone will forget about the failure of the Miami club."

Julie winched. "We don't say failure. We say setback."

A big setback in the case of their small firm. They had started strong, opening successful nightclubs in

Atlanta, Charlotte and Nashville. The name Dominant Development was garnering respect until the Miami nightclub. Crash-and-burn failure was an understatement. The place hadn't stayed open for six months before fights between rival gangs and rumors of drug trafficking shut it down. Julie had been leery of working with the newly rich rapper who had wanted the club, but the guy was at the top of the charts at the time, and she'd fallen back on her *go all in or go home* rule. Regardless of how well her other nightclubs were doing, the disaster that was the Miami club is what people were talking about now.

"Setback, failure, call it what you want. We need another big opening," Evette said.

"Yes, but we also just landed two new clients, and those projects are going to take a lot of effort. We are on the verge of needing one more agent."

Evette raised her pointer and middle fingers. "Two."

"Fine, we need two more people to handle the workload. It's not a good time for me to hop on a plane and fly across the country to open a new nightclub."

Evette took a deep breath, which meant she was trying hard to think about Julie's arguments instead of just blowing her off. "I hear what you're saying, but I think this is the perfect time. If you open a nightclub associated with Raymond, and it's successful, it will wash away the mess that was Miami and get us in the playing field on the West Coast. The jerks at Nexon-Jones will lose their minds. Isn't this why you started this place?"

No truer words were spoken. After leaving Nexon-Jones, Raymond had introduced her to rapper Antwan Harmon, who went by just Antwan. Her attraction to

Antwan was immediate; she'd fallen for his swagger and intensity, and was even a little thrilled by his street appeal. When he'd stopped talking with Nexon-Jones about opening a club in Atlanta and trusted her to open the place instead, she'd fallen in love. She'd stolen a major client from her former employer and found the man she'd spend the rest of her life with. The former thought had worked out, the latter not so much. Opening night, she'd found out she was just one of many women in love with Antwan.

Her heartbreak was coupled with the knowledge that her former boss started spreading the word that she'd only landed Antwan's account because she was sleeping with him. She'd also heard that some blamed her for making the decision about the Miami club because of her "relationship" with the client. Now she made sure to keep a very wide distance between her and any person she worked for.

"I'd feel guilty if I left you alone in the midst of this."

"Girl, quit being crazy. We've already narrowed down the agents we want to interview. I'll handle bringing on the new agents."

"I wanted to be involved."

"Why? You don't trust my judgment?" Evette asked without any indication that she believed the statement.

"Of course I do," Julie said with sincerity. She trusted Evette more than anyone. "If this pans out, I'll be out there for several months, at least until the club is opened."

"You can come back once or twice a month if it gets really crazy back here. Let go of some of that control freak, and go get us more business. Besides, isn't the point of having a famous friend is so he can help you out?"

"Says who?"

"Says me. Let your friendship with Raymond be useful for once."

Julie chuckled and leaned back in the chair. "I don't know why you dislike him so much. Raymond has been a great friend. He helped me out when I was turning into a poor, sad basket case. He taught me how to—"

"Guard your heart," Evette finished with a hand wave. "I know. You and those crazy dating rules."

"They aren't crazy. I got caught up in that relationship with Antwan and thought there was more to us than there was. You remember how pathetic I was. If it weren't for Raymond schooling me on the way men think, I would've fallen for more pitiful lines and believed I was in a relationship with a guy when I was actually a booty call."

"Raymond's so-called education—" Evette made air quotes with her fingers "—has given you a convenient excuse to keep men at arm's length."

"I date." Julie shrugged. "Guys love me. Unfortunately, they love me for all the wrong reasons."

The few celebrity men she met were just as conceited and into playing games as Antwan. She preferred dating men outside the entertainment industry. Sadly, the few she had dated either played the same games or thought she was a good route to meeting famous people.

"Guys love trying to break through the wall you've surrounded yourself with. You're a challenge."

"Which is ten times better than being an easy conquest."

"I still think Raymond's education is just a way for him to keep you single."

This time Julie waved away Evette's words. "We're just friends, Evette. For the hundredth time, Raymond only gives advice on men when I ask for it, and he's spot-on every time. He's not keeping me single—the lack of available men is keeping me single."

Evette grunted. "I can't argue with that. Anyway, back to my original point. If Raymond wants you to oversee opening his nightclub—regardless of how busy we are here—I think you should go. At least see what his plans are and make sure it's worth our time."

"There's one more little thing."

"What's that?"

Julie studied her perfectly polished nails. "He's opening the place with Dante Wilson." Her voice was blasé when she knew this news would shatter any sense of calm Evette had.

Evette slapped her desk with both hands, her eyes as wide as saucers. "Dante Wilson?" Julie nodded. "*The* Dante Wilson? Mr. I Can Sing, Dance and Play a Dozen Instruments Dante Wilson? Dante Wilson of W. M. Records, whose parents, grandparents and great-grandparents were music legends?"

Julie chuckled. "The one and same."

Evette pointed at Julie. "You're getting on that plane, today, and you're checking out this lead. Why didn't you say that first?"

"Because I didn't want it to sway your decision. This is huge, but if you had any hesitation about handling the two new accounts, hiring new staff and our current projects while I was on the West Coast, I would have said no."

Evette took another deep breath. "Julie, I appreciate you thinking of me, seriously, but if you are not in Malibu by the end of the week, I swear I'm going to strangle you." Her calm tone gave way to excitement by the end of the sentence.

Julie grinned and stood. "No need for violence. I'll go back to my office and finally click Submit."

"On what?"

"The purchase of the plane ticket I started buying before coming in here."

Chapter 3

Julie sat in the backseat of the car Raymond had waiting for her at the airport and reviewed the list of reputable contractors in and around Malibu, California. Paying attention to the details instead of taking in the beautiful sights along the Pacific Coast Highway was proving difficult for her. Between the awe-inspiring mountains and sparkling sea, she really wished she was there for pleasure instead of business. But business was the reason she'd left Evette in Atlanta, so she tore her eyes away from the views and scanned contractor websites.

Picking contractors before actually being vetted as Raymond and Dante's final partner was presumptuous. Raymond basically wanted her to come and talk about possibly working with them. She'd mainly gotten her jobs by acting as if she already had them. The tactic hadn't failed her yet.

Later, when the car pulled down one of the gated entrances that she assumed blocked the way to the homes of Hollywood's rich and famous, her stomach churned like the waves against the bluffs she'd admired on the drive up. She was actually about to meet Dante Wilson. Thanks to her friendship with Raymond and her work opening popular nightclubs, she wasn't easily starstruck. However, she'd listened to and loved Dante's music for most of her life. From her preteens through her bad breakup with Antwan, the guy always had a song on the radio rotation that seemed to fit the mood of her life.

She'd dressed nicely for her flight. Albeit her black trousers, white cowl-neck blouse and tailored red blazer were travel worn, she still looked casual but professional. While the driver announced their arrival at the gate, Julie pulled out her compact to double-check her makeup and smooth her hand down the back of her stylish pixie cut.

The gates opened, and the driver maneuvered the car down the long drive and parked in front of a huge stone villa. She would have been impressed by the house and its magnificent views if not for the obvious signs of a party going on. She frowned in confusion when the driver opened the door, where she was greeted by music coming from the back, along with laughter and voices. Three women in skimpy bikinis and two men in board shorts stood out front. Another car pulled up, and the group got in.

She glanced at the driver. "Are we at the right place?"

"Yes, ma'am. This is Dante Wilson's residence."

Julie nodded, then turned back to the sounds of revelry coming from the villa. She crossed the stone-tiled

entrance to the front door. Julie rang the doorbell, un-
sure if the chime would even be heard over the sounds
of the party. Hell, did she even need to ring the bell?

A guy wearing blue-and-red swim trunks opened
the door. "Hey, come on in," he said, waving her inside.

Julie thanked him, entered the home and immediately felt overdressed. Men in swim trunks and women
in bathing suits filled the house. The main area, with
tan stone walls, dark walnut floors, modern furnishings
and expensive decorations, was completely open to the
outside, where a crystal-blue infinity pool overlooked
the ocean. Even more people in bathing suits milled
around the expansive outdoor living space.

"Are you here for the party?" the guy asked.

"Umm, I'm meeting with Raymond," she said.

"Oh, come on—he's out by the pool."

Julie followed him through the crowd out to the
pool. "He's there." He pointed.

Raymond was in the middle of the pool, playing
water polo with several bikini-clad women. Of course
he would be. Julie rolled her eyes, but she smiled despite her disappointment that he wasn't prepared for a
real meeting. Raymond would never change. They'd
met freshmen year in college at a party. Though she'd
flirted with him, she'd turned down his attempts to get
her in bed. She'd never felt that way about Raymond.
Eventually, their flirty relationship had become a close
friendship by the time they graduated and Raymond's
music career kicked off. She knew if there was a party
to attend or a good-looking woman to get with, Raymond was there.

Still, as she stood by the pool, sweltering in a blazer
while everyone else was clad in swimwear, a strong

pull of annoyance that Raymond hadn't mentioned she would be walking into a pool party and not a business meeting swept through her. She really hoped he wasn't wasting her time. She loved Raymond like a brother, but she wouldn't hesitate to wring his neck if he pulled her away from Atlanta over a whim of his.

"Hey, Raymond," she called. Her voice, and the annoyance in it, carried above the music and female laughter.

Raymond turned away from the game to look her way. His grin widened. "Julie!" he exclaimed with slight surprise.

She worked very hard not to roll her eyes again. The volleyball hit him in the side of the head, and a chorus of chuckles came up from the various women in the pool.

Raymond shook his head and blinked several times. "I'm coming out now." He swam to the edge of the pool and pulled himself out of the water. Every woman in the pool eyed his muscular body with desire and enthusiasm—chiseled muscles beneath smooth tan skin, a pretty-boy face with green eyes to boot. Julie understood their admiration, though she didn't share their desire.

He took a few steps to her and tried to hug her. Julie jumped back and held up a hand. "No way, you're soaking wet."

Raymond's eyes flashed with mischief that Julie knew all too well. "I'm serious, Raymond—this is a new blazer, and you can't mess it up with a chlorine-filled hug."

He chuckled and edged closer. "I haven't seen you in ages, and you won't hug me because of a jacket."

Julie took a step back. "No, I won't hug you, but I do feel like punching you."

That stopped his movement. "What did I do this time?"

Julie raised a brow and looked around. "Ray, I thought we were meeting to discuss business. Instead you're having a party."

"Oh, that," he said with a shrug. "We can still talk." He waved over a woman lounging nearby. The beauty stood and brought him a towel. "Thanks, baby." Raymond slapped her behind as she walked away, then wiped the excess water from his face.

"You know, I'd rather talk when you're not in the middle of an orgy. I'll check into the hotel, and we can meet up tomorrow."

She'd booked the hotel suite for a month with plans to extend that or possibly rent someplace if it seemed the club opening would take a long time. If it fell through, she would make Raymond pay any hotel cancellation fees.

"No! Sorry, Julie, this party just kind of happened."

Julie doubted that. There were too many people here for the party to *kind of* happen, but she kept that thought to herself. "All the more reason to wait until we can really talk about things."

"Seriously, we can. Dante is here. I told him you were coming today."

Julie glanced around at the people present. She recognized some celebrities and reality stars, but Dante wasn't in the mix.

"He's inside," Raymond said. "Come on. At least say hello, since you got all dressed to impress, and then stay and relax for a while."

"Raymond, I'm here on business, not to relax."

"Not all business is handled in a boardroom, Julie. Chill out for a second and come meet Dante."

He took her hand and gently tugged her toward the door. Julie twisted her lip but let him lead her. Honestly, she shouldn't be surprised that Raymond asked her to meet him to discuss business at the same time Dante "accidentally" threw a party. His fun personality and spontaneity were part of the persona that had turned him into a star.

"How was your flight? Did the driver get to the airport on time? I gave him your arrival and told him to be there on time." Raymond fired off the questions.

Julie answered those and the half-dozen others Raymond threw her way as they walked through the crowded living area toward the back of the house. His questions reminded her of their college days when he always worried about her walking across campus at night by herself. His concern for her welfare was why she'd eventually viewed him as a brother. His concern grew after her breakup with Antwan. She knew Raymond blamed himself for introducing her to the guy, and she believed that was why he was so forthcoming with her about all the sleazy ways men thought and the tricks they pulled.

In the back of the house, the sounds of the party were replaced by the sound of piano music along with Dante's smooth tenor singing.

"Let me hold you in my arms. Let me comfort you all night long. Let me be the man to kiss away your fears."

Julie's heart ached as the words took her back to the time after the Antwan breakup when she'd listened to this song and yearned for a guy to be all those things. She'd listened to the song repeatedly. She hated herself for moping so much over a man who didn't deserve it, and hearing Dante sing stirred up the longing she'd thought was long gone.

She and Raymond stopped at the open door of the room where the music came from. A large grand piano stood in the center of what she could see was a music room with other instruments, framed albums and pictures of the Wilson family lining the walls. Dante sat behind the piano; four women in colorful bikinis surrounded him like beautiful birds. She hadn't listened to the song in ages. His voice swept her up in thoughts of how nice having a man actually kiss away her fears would be.

She'd known Dante was handsome and that he could sing, but to witness his talent and his beauty up close and personal took her breath away.

His eyes were closed, and the flash of his perfect white teeth gleamed between lips that made her think of marathon rounds of kissing, touching and sexing. His head swayed gently back and forth to the sound of the music. His curly dark hair was tapered at the sides and thicker on the top. A dusting of hair covered his square jaw. Julie's gaze slid over wide shoulders in a white shirt unbuttoned just enough to give a glimpse of a smooth muscled chest and warm brown skin. As if she were still standing beneath the sun, Julie's body burned. Her nipples hardened, and a slow, sultry heat that matched the smoldering sound of Dante's voice slid through her body.

Julie shifted from one foot to the other. This was not good. She could not be attracted to him. She tried to ignore her primal response, but the concentration of heat between her thighs continued in a mocking *sucks for you* kind of way.

The music stopped, and no one spoke until the last note drifted away. Dante opened his eyes, and the ladies clapped and squealed their praise. His lips spread in a wide-open grin. His sexy dark eyes sparkled with a look that made a woman want to forget every lesson about acting like a lady. A sound, part whimper, part suppressed giggle, rang in her ear; a second later, she realized she'd made the sound.

Raymond shifted beside her. Dante looked up, his dark gaze connecting with hers so hard she gasped out the little bit of air that remained in her chest. *Oh, hell, I'm screwed.*

"Raymond," Dante said, his very interested eyes still on Julie, "please introduce your beautiful friend."

Chapter 4

Dante's smile widened as the woman with Raymond snapped her mouth closed and lifted her chin. He didn't miss the blatant desire burning in her wonderful light brown eyes before she'd hidden the emotion behind a professional mask. His gaze slowly traced over her body, and his abdomen tightened with anticipation. Forgetting the beauties who'd dragged him to the music room, and the fun he'd planned to have with them, Dante stood and crossed the room.

He took in more of her appearance the closer he got. He liked everything he saw: short, stylish hair highlighted blond, the bangs just long enough to brush arched brows; clear, direct amber eyes; and a full, sensuous mouth. Her black pants didn't hug her curves, but the material didn't hide her shapely figure either. The red blazer brought attention to her waist and the scooped neckline of her shirt drew his eyes to her sexy cleavage. Sexy cherry-red heels brought her to almost his height.

"Dante," Raymond said. "This is Julie Dominick."

Dante held out his hand. "Julie Dominick." He said her name slowly, enjoying the sound. "It's very nice to meet you."

He took her hand and kissed the back, catching a whiff of her perfume. The warm scent brought to mind dark rooms and Julie sliding across satin sheets beneath him.

"It's a pleasure meeting you, Dante," she said, and she didn't pull her hand away. "Out of all your songs, that is my favorite."

Her gaze was straightforward—no batting lashes or shy glances. He liked that immediately. She was a woman who wasn't hesitant. Despite her directness, that hot spark from when their eyes first met was nowhere to be seen. He wanted the spark back.

"I'd be happy to sing it for you anytime you'd like."

Her smile tipped up at the corners, and she slowly slid her hand out of his. The gentle glide of her slim fingers sent shivers down his arm. "Raymond didn't tell me you were having a party. I expected a business meeting."

She'd ignored his obvious flirtation, which meant she was going to try to ignore what he'd noticed and felt between them. He should do the same, but direct and beautiful women were his weakness.

"A friend came over, and before we knew it there was a houseful of people. The whole party happened on a whim."

"Hmm, is opening your club also due to a whim?"

She looked from Dante to Raymond. He heard the insinuation that they were wasting her time. Dante grinned. Direct, beautiful and bold. Ballsy for a woman trying to go into business with him. He liked her even more, even if he didn't like the assumption that he wasn't serious about opening the club.

"I promise you, I'm very serious about the opening of my club. I'd like to debut new artists under my own label there. My family wouldn't support these artists at venues owned and managed by W. M. Records."

Her brows rose. He'd surprised her.

"Then I'll do everything I can to make sure this place opens smoothly."

Raymond smiled at them both. "I'm telling you, Dante, Julie is the right person for the job."

His body was definitely on board with Julie handling this project, but his brain interjected. This was important to him for multiple reasons; he couldn't just go with the decision the head below his belt was trying to get him to make.

"We'll see. I'm talking to a few other developers."

The corner of her inviting lips lifted, and her head tilted to the side. "Talk to them all you want. I know I'm the right person. In the next few days, you'll know it, too."

Dante added "confident" to the things about Julie Dominick that were making ignoring the head below his belt harder.

One of the women from the piano came over. "Are you ready to sing for us again?" she asked with a bright smile.

Julie stepped back. "I mentioned to Raymond that I

can come back tomorrow to discuss business. I'm more than happy to do that."

Raymond placed a hand on her arm. "Don't leave, Julie."

Dante zeroed in on Raymond's hands on Julie, so familiar, without a bit of hesitation or awkwardness between them. Raymond said nothing was going on between him and Julie, but he'd also said she was the woman he could consider settling down with later, which meant Dante should pull back. No matter how his body reacted to her, he shouldn't step on Raymond's toes that way.

"Stay," Dante said. "Change and join the party."

She shook her head. "I'm not prepared for a pool party."

Raymond chuckled. "You can't tell me you came to Malibu and didn't bring a swimsuit. Get the thing out, and come sit by the pool. I know this is a business trip, but you can have a few minutes to enjoy yourself."

She glanced at Dante, and he nodded. He may not step on Raymond's toes, but that didn't mean he didn't want her to stick around so he could see her in a bathing suit. Maybe the desire caused by that thought showed in his expression because the spark he'd witnessed earlier made a brief appearance in Julie's eyes. It was quickly hidden when she turned to Raymond. "Fine. I'll change and join you."

Raymond dragged Julie away to get her bags and showed her where to change. Dante would have preferred to do that himself, but she was Raymond's friend. Better for Dante to keep his distance.

He sang another song for the ladies in the music room but wasn't really into having fun with them anymore, so he ushered them back to the pool. They kept him company, and he listened to them talk about inconsequential things. Each one tried to gain his attention and figure out who he'd spend the rest of the day with. It was a question he'd been debating before Julie walked through the door and broke his thoughts, scattering them like balls on a pool table.

The source of the scattering came out onto the patio, Raymond with her. Dante took a sip of beer that stuck in his throat. He coughed and sat up in his chair. Julie in a business suit was a man's fantasy; Julie in a bathing suit was a man's erotic dream. The red one-piece suit was plastered to full breasts and a flat stomach. It rose high on her hips; no sarong or wrap hid the perfection of her thighs and legs. Confident with a capital *C*. She'd switched the heels for a pair of red sandals. Dante took another gulp of his beer to stop his groan of appreciation from escaping.

She and Raymond settled into chairs across the pool. They talked and laughed, looking every bit the close friends Raymond said they were. She glanced around the space. Her gaze stopped several times as she took in the various people. When she stopped on him, a small smile lifted her lips and made his heart jump before she continued her perusal. What did that smile mean? Did she feel the same knocked-out-of-breath feeling when their eyes met, or was she just smiling at a potential business partner she had to acknowledge? He couldn't say she was looking only for him because she seemed to check out everyone there.

He ran a hand over his face. *What the hell?* When did he become the guy obsessing over what a woman was thinking? Julie's closeness with Raymond meant he had to keep his hands to himself. If she did get the job, getting involved with her might cloud his judgment about the club. He should ignore her.

A woman that Raymond had hooked up with came over to him and Julie. Raymond introduced her. Julie smiled and held out her hand. Dante noted her friendly and jealous-free greeting. The woman clung to Raymond's side. After a few minutes of talking, Julie waved Raymond and the woman away. They strolled toward the door. Julie watched them, but there was no hint of regret, anger or disappointment on her face. *Okay, maybe they are just friends.*

Her eyes lifted and met his. Dante's heart danced behind his rib cage. Again, she gave him a small smile, then looked away. He was up and out of the chair in an instant.

"I'll have to tell Raymond to never leave a beautiful woman alone at a party," he said as he sat next to her. "Someone else may slip in."

Her smile was good-natured, not flirtatious. "Actually, I was waiting for him to leave. He has a way of unintentionally blocking. Now I'm free to talk with whomever I want."

Dante liked the sound of that. "Really?"

"Yeah."

"Anyone here you're interested in having a conversation with?"

Her smile made him hot all over. "Actually, there is a guy I wouldn't mind talking to."

Dante's grin widened. He slid his arm across the back of the chair and moved closer. "I'd love to know who."

She looked over his shoulder, then used her head

to indicate behind Dante. "Him. The guy in the green trunks."

Dante frowned and glanced around. Carlos, the drummer they'd had to call in on the last leg of the tour after Dante's original drummer got sick, stood on the other side of the pool. There was something about Carlos that Dante didn't really like, but he'd chalked his feelings up to his dislike of unexpected changes. Carlos played well and hadn't caused any problems on tour, so Dante ignored his weird feelings toward the guy.

"Him?"

"You sound surprised," she said, and he swore amusement filled her voice.

"I thought you might be interested in someone else."

"Really, who?"

There was definite humor in her amber eyes.

"I thought you'd want to spend more time with Raymond."

She shook her head, then crossed her long and shapely legs. "Oh. Not really. Ray and I have plenty of time to catch up while I'm working with you two."

Spoken as if she already had the job. "Him leaving with another woman didn't bother you?"

Her eyes sparkled with amusement and she waved a hand. "That. No. I've known Ray way too long to get upset when he ditches me for another female."

"Did it used to bother you?"

She shook her head. "No. Ray is cool, but I know him too well to fall for him."

"That's good to know."

"Why? Did you think my relationship with him would compromise my ability to do the job?"

"I just like to be sure."

"You can be sure. I don't mix business with pleasure, and I never date partners."

He leaned in and stared into her beautiful eyes. "I'm sure exceptions can be made."

Her smirk was cute, and the twist of her full lips made him want to kiss her. "Ray and I are not worth an exception."

Dante rubbed his chin. "What if I'm the exception?"

A spark flashed in the depths of her eyes. She shifted, then looked away. When she looked back at him, the spark was gone, all interest hidden.

"I'll admit I used to drool over your posters in my music magazines when I was a teen. You once occupied a fair amount of space in my fantasies, but that was fifteen years ago. Girlish fantasies gave way to adult responsibilities."

He leaned forward until only a few inches separated them. "Forget the girlish fantasies. I want to be a part of your very grown-up thoughts."

She held his gaze for what felt like hours. Despite the neutral expression on her face, he noticed her quick inhale. The rhythm of excitement he got when pursuing a new woman quickened his pulse.

Her brows rose, and her head tilted to the side. "Have brunch with me tomorrow. I'll tell you about my grown-up thoughts." There was no flirtation in her voice; she sounded almost businesslike, but the humor remained in her eyes.

Dante wasn't sure what that meant, but he wasn't about to deny a chance to be with her tomorrow. "I know a place."

She shook her head. "I've already looked up local restaurants, and I'd like to go to Geoffrey's. I'll meet you there at nine."

This woman knew what she wanted, meaning she was going to be damn difficult to resist. "I'll be there."

Her devilish smile made him feel as if he were missing something. "It's a date." She stood and walked away.

Dante watched the sexy sway of her hips, his body hardening with each one of her assertive steps. His desire was quickly doused when she crossed over to speak with Carlos.

What the...? Women didn't typically leave him to talk to another man. For the first time, he'd been thrown off by a woman.

Julie shifted her position next to Carlos, and her gaze flitted to Dante for a second. Dante grinned and leaned back in the chair. Her quick look got him back on balance. Julie Dominick may play impartial toward him, but she was interested. He couldn't step to Raymond's girl like that, but he damn sure was going to enjoy the heat sizzling between them.

Chapter 5

Julie casually sipped ice water and stared out at the magnificent ocean view from the patio at Geoffrey's Malibu. Immediately after booking her trip, she'd looked into places that would work for relaxed business meetings and that offered superb food. As she looked over the brunch menu, she was pleased with her choice.

After putting down the water, she pulled out her tablet and navigated to the website of the contractor she was considering hiring for the club. The sun was hot, and she wore a sleeveless beige blouse with a tan pencil skirt, so she wasn't sweltering like yesterday. She leaned forward to get more shade from the white umbrella over the table to see the screen better. She'd gotten a list of reputable contractors from the coworkers who didn't hate her for her abrupt exit from Nexon-Jones. She'd narrowed her choices down to three firms, and, depending on their availability, along with Dante's and Raymond's schedules, she hoped to have one secured by the end of the week.

"She's right here, Mr. Wilson." The host's voice came from behind Julie.

She glanced up from the tablet to where the young man indicated to her. Dante smiled and thanked the host, looking every bit the sex symbol that he was in a fitted dark gray T-shirt, white pants and dark shoes. Julie swallowed hard and sucked in a breath. The man had thrown her off yesterday. She'd assumed Dante would be charming, flirtatious even, but when he'd indicated that he should be the exception to her no-mixing-business-and-pleasure rule, her mind became slushy.

How badly she'd wanted to take him up on that offer was almost embarrassing. Getting involved with a guy in the entertainment industry, and a business partner at that, went against many of the rules that prevented her from being played by a man.

"Good afternoon," she said with what she envisioned to be a professional, I'm-not-drooling-internally smile.

"You're early." He pulled out a chair and sat down.

"I'm typically early when I have a meeting."

He raised a brow and placed his forearms on the table. The breeze brought over the scent of the sea and his enticing cologne. Dante leaned closer to her. "Meeting. I thought this was a date?"

She had left him with that impression, and she had to admit, there were plenty of things worse than going on a date with him. Too bad for him. She wasn't here to have a fling with Dante or jeopardize her reputation.

But she would flirt. Flirting went a lot further and

got her a lot more than being an ice-cold superbitch.
From what she knew about men, flirting was just another tactic they used to throw a woman off her game.

"This isn't a date," she said with a smile.

"You promised to give a little insight on your very
adult thoughts."

The way he said "adult thoughts" had her imagining all types of adult things—things that involved him,
naked and smiling.

Julie leaned back in her chair. "Are you sure you're
ready to hear them?"

"Oh, I'm very sure."

"I'm glad to hear that. Because I've thought about
this all morning." She leaned forward.

Excitement entered his eyes. "You have?"

"All night, honestly. I can't get the thoughts out of
my mind."

"Sometimes talking about things helps, or having
a helping hand." His warm hand covered hers. The
touch nearly made her forget this was supposed to be
harmless flirting.

"Are you willing to help?"

"In any way possible."

"I thought you would be." She glanced down at his
long fingers casually brushing the back of her hand.
Each light stroke was like a dose of steroids to her
pumped-up hormones. "You've got nice hands."

"They're willing to help you in any way."

The muscles of her thighs clenched. Julie pulled her
hand away. *Time to remember this is supposed to be
harmless flirting.* "Good, because I'm meeting with a
contractor that I'm considering hiring to help with the

renovation of the building you've picked out for the club. I'd like to get your opinion."

His smile froze for a second before his brows drew together. "Excuse me?"

"I've narrowed the choices down to three, and, of course, I won't pick one without discussing the details with you and Raymond first. I'm glad you're so willing to help."

"So that's why you invited me here?"

"Of course. Why else would I?" She tried to look innocent but knew he had to see the humor in her expression. She was having a hard time not chuckling at his confusion.

Julie quickly turned and nearly sagged with relief when she saw the hostess bringing the contractor to their table. She stood and held out her hand to the man beside the hostess.

"Orlando Salvatore," she said.

Orlando nodded and took her hand. He was tall with wavy dark hair, gleaming straight teeth and a body honed from working in construction. His white shirt and dark brown pants accentuated broad shoulders and strong legs.

"And you must be Julie Dominick." His handshake was firm but not too tight.

"I am. Thank you for meeting me this morning."

"No problem at all. I'd love to work on this project."

Julie grinned, then held out her hand to Dante, who watched her with slightly narrowed eyes. "He needs no introduction, but this is Dante Wilson. Obviously, he'll be involved with choosing the contractor for the job."

"Of course," Orlando said. "It's very nice to meet you, Mr. Wilson. I'm a big fan."

Dante slowly stood and shook Orlando's hand. "Flattery will get you everywhere."

Orlando grinned. "I only speak the truth."

Julie sat, and then Orlando and Dante followed suit. Julie ignored Dante's direct gaze on her. Outwardly, anyway. Inside, her body was a ball of nerves. She hoped to impress Dante with her proactive approach to handling the development of the nightclub. It was the reason she'd invited him here this morning. *Go hard or go home.*

"I've been looking at your website, Orlando," Julie said. "I'm impressed with the jobs you've handled. I see that you've also been chosen to open a nightclub in LA. Will you be able to handle another job?"

She didn't like small talk and preferred going directly into any concerns. She trusted the recommendation she'd gotten from her former coworker, but she couldn't forget he still worked for Nexon-Jones.

Orlando handled her direct question easily and went right into the number of crews he had working for him and how he scheduled his workload. He answered all Julie's questions easily and impressively while they waited on their food. Dante perked up and stopped glaring at her long enough to ask Orlando some of his own questions. From the interest and satisfaction that flashed on Dante's face, she guessed he was also impressed by Orlando.

By the end of the meal, her questions were done. After a few minutes of small talk, Julie wrapped up the meeting.

"Thank you again for meeting with me, Orlando," Julie said. "I'll be in touch before the end of the week."

She stood and so did the men. Orlando shook Dante's

hand, then hers. When she would have pulled back, he held on. "The pleasure was all mine. I hope to hear from you soon, regardless of the outcome."

Orlando's smile and the flirtatious tone were clear. Julie returned his smile with one of her own and nodded. "I'll be sure to give you a call."

"Do that," Orlando said before leaving.

Dante looked at Orlando's retreating back and then at Julie. "What was that?"

"What was what?" Julie sat back down.

Dante sat and motioned his head in Orlando's direction. "That?"

"That was me thinking I've found our contractor. Didn't you like him?"

"He was all right."

"All right? Did you look at the work he's done, all on time? That's big when it comes to contractors. Of course, I'm going to check his references."

"You're ready to hire him already?"

"He was my top choice, but we've got another interview later today."

His brows rose. "We do?"

"Yeah." She checked her watch. "I agreed to meet her for a late lunch. Are you available?"

"Her?"

Julie raised a brow. "Do you have a problem with a woman?"

He raised his hands. "Not at all. At least this time you won't spend the meeting grinning and giggling over the guy."

"I don't giggle."

"Yes, you do." He quirked a brow. "It would be cute. If you were giggling over me."

She laughed. "Still want me to make you my exception to the no-business-and-pleasure-mixing rule?"

"I'd like to know if you were considering it."

She eyed him from head to toe. "I've already considered it."

"And?"

"And you're talented, sexy and very smug. I'm not interested."

Dante rubbed his jaw. "If you would have let this be a real date, I think you would be. I envisioned this morning going a lot differently."

"What did you envision?"

"Brunch, sightseeing, maybe a kiss."

She glanced at his lips, imagined them on hers and was hit with a wave of longing, which she quickly pushed aside. "I'm here to work. I promise—I will not be kissing you."

"I believe that not only will we kiss but that you'll initiate it." He looked so arrogant and sure of himself that, for a second, her heart trembled, and she believed he might be right.

Chapter 6

Dante met up with Raymond at the end of the week at a jazz club in Los Angeles. When he wasn't on tour or working on an album, Dante preferred the laid-back atmosphere of his villa in Malibu over the constant hustle of LA, unless there was a party worth attending. Tonight there was a huge party planned after Jacobe's basketball game. Dante never refused a chance to party.

He found Raymond in the club's VIP section, watching a lovely and curvy woman singing onstage. They'd agreed to meet here before going to the game and then the party. After sitting in an interview with another contractor and Julie that morning, and after she'd made it obvious, yet again, that she wasn't giving him any play, Dante was more than ready to spend the night partying.

Dante strolled over and sat next to Raymond. "What's up with your girl?"

Raymond raised a brow. "Who?"

"Julie."

Raymond grinned and sipped on the drink in his hand. "Nothing, she's just trying to do a good job."

"When did we officially make her a partner?"

Raymond chuckled. "We didn't. Julie always tackles a job like she's got it. By the time she's finished putting the pieces together, people wonder why they wouldn't partner with her."

Dante was in that exact predicament. She had pulled together the best contractors in the area and drilled them on their ability to perform. After seeing her in action, he wondered why he should look for anyone else.

"She knows her stuff. I thought we were meeting for brunch the other day, and she's setting up interviews with potential contractors."

Raymond frowned. "You met her for brunch? When?"

"Tuesday. I thought you knew?"

"I knew she was checking out some contractors but not that she was meeting with you to do that."

Dante leaned back on the black couch and spread his arms across the back. "I thought she had agreed to a date."

Raymond sat up straight and put his drink on the table. "You asked her on a date?"

"After you left her at the pool to hang out with that other woman, I didn't think you'd have a problem."

"Why didn't you tell me you *thought* you were going out with her? I told you about us."

Dante raised a hand. "Hold up. Us—what us? She was at the party for a second, and you walked away with another woman."

Raymond slid forward on the chair and tugged on

his black leather pants before holding out his hands. "That woman from the party doesn't mean anything. Julie is the one. The one I'm going to settle down with. After I finish, you know." Raymond popped his collar. "Enjoying myself."

"What makes you think she's going to want to settle down with you after you finish sleeping with half of the female population?"

"Because of the pact we made in college. If we're both single, then we'll get together."

"So you think she's just going to sit around being single waiting on that day to come?"

"She has so far," Raymond said smugly. "Julie hasn't gotten serious about any guy since getting her heart broken a few years back. I was the guy who helped her get through that. We would have hooked up then, but, you know, my career was just starting. She said she didn't want to hold me back or make me keep promises. So we agreed to be friends."

"Why does that make you so sure she's waiting for the day you two can finally be together?"

Raymond grinned and sat back in his chair. He crossed one ankle over the opposite knee, the epitome of someone used to getting his way. "Whenever I need her, she's there. Don't get me wrong—I'm there for her, too. We're cool. She doesn't bug me about the women I date, but she still calls me when she's having trouble figuring out a man's she's with. I give her advice."

Dante's eyes narrowed. "What type of advice?"

"I tell her rules that men date by. Then she ends up calling a dude on his crap, breaks things off and lets me know that, yet again, I helped her out."

"You're sabotaging her relationships."

Raymond shook his head. "No. I tell her what men think. Julie's smart enough to figure out the rest. Every once in a while she meets a decent fellow, and I tell her that. In the end, she breaks up with them." Raymond smiled. "Now you understand?"

"Understand what?"

"She's breaking up with ratchet dudes and good dudes. She's waiting on us."

"I see that you're keeping her waiting in the wings. Besides, I don't think she sees things the same way you're seeing them. She says she's not interested in you."

"What's she supposed to say? 'I'm waiting for the day that Raymond and I can finally be together'?"

Dante knew no woman would admit to holding a torch for one guy for years, but he didn't believe that was the case with Julie. He'd watched her and Raymond. Granted, it was just one time, but he could tell a lot about what a woman was thinking by watching her. Julie had been happy to see her friend but also annoyed there was a party going on instead of a business meeting. She hadn't watched Raymond with any sense of longing, and no telltale signs of desire or attraction popped up when they were together. If anything, Dante figured Julie had listened to Raymond's advice enough to know he was trying to keep her waiting in the wings. Maybe she was doing the same with Raymond, letting him think there was a chance one day so that she could still rely on her friend when she needed him.

Or maybe you don't want to believe she's really not interested in you.

"I take it that you're telling me this because you want me to stay away from Julie," Dante said.

"I'd prefer it if you would. I really like Julie, and while I don't think she'll fall for you, it would be weird later when she and I get together for you two to have history."

"Do you really like her, or are you just trying to hold on to her?"

The smug look left Raymond's face. "I do really like her. She's beautiful, hardworking and confident. I've only seen Julie cry once in the years I've known her. *Once*. You know how often women like to throw around tears. I've had a crush on her for years, have wanted to get with her just as long, but the timing is never right. If we would have hooked up back when she was hurt, it would have worked for a while but not long."

"Why not?"

"You know how life is on the road. Before I blew up, I could count on one hand the number of women I'd slept with. I hit that same number in one night after my single hit number one. I want Julie, but I don't want to hurt her either." Raymond picked up his drink and turned to the stage.

Dante frowned and also watched the woman performing. If it wasn't for the earnestness in Raymond's tone, Dante would have called bull. Instead he understood Raymond's logic. Life as a celebrity was nothing but constant temptation. He'd had girls and, at times, grown women throwing panties at him when he was only thirteen. One of the reasons he hadn't settled down was because of that. He didn't rule out *maybe* getting married one day. If he could find what his parents had that made them stay together despite the enticements. He just hadn't found the woman who got him feeling that way yet. He was sure that the love he sang about existed, and that he'd know it when he found it.

"I'll respect your wishes," Dante said, the words burning his tongue. Raymond was his boy, and he wouldn't do that to his boy.

"Thanks, man," Raymond said.

The woman onstage stopped singing. She looked at Raymond, who grinned and waved her over.

"Did you invite Julie to the game and after-party tonight?" Dante asked. If Raymond knew he would one day marry her, Dante figured he would be trying to spend as much time with her as possible.

"Nah, I told her I'd give her a call tomorrow. She said she was tired after the meetings today."

"You two could just hang out."

Raymond smiled at the singer walking over. "I've got another woman meeting me at the party. Besides, she mentioned Carlos called to ask her to dinner. I think she's going out with him."

Jealousy and anger flared up in Dante. "And you don't care?"

Raymond shook his head. He stood as the singer entered the VIP area. "We ain't together yet. Carlos is just another date, and definitely no threat to me. He won't mean anything." Raymond ran his hand up the arm of the singer and gave her a seductive smile. "You want to come back to my place?"

The woman grinned. "Of course."

Dante shook his head. Was this dude serious? "Raymond, what about the game?"

Raymond waved Dante's words off. "I'll be at the after-party."

"Do you even know where he's taking her?" Dante asked.

Raymond paused in the middle of taking the woman out of the VIP. "Who?"

"Carlos," Dante bit out, trying hard to hide his frustration with Raymond. "What if this guy is crazy?"

Raymond smirked and looked at Dante. "Julie can handle herself. Even if I were concerned, they're going to that new sunset restaurant on the PCH. There will be so many people there, nothing can go wrong."

Raymond put his arm around the woman and led her toward the door. Dante watched them, his jaw clenched. He'd listened to Raymond spout off about wanting to be with Julie. Maybe Raymond even believed some of his own bull. However, Dante was absolutely certain about one thing. Despite how much Raymond had gotten it into his head that he and Julie belonged together, they didn't. Dante doubted Julie wanted Raymond, and he damn sure knew that if Raymond really wanted to be with Julie one day, he wouldn't be asking another woman back to his LA condo before meeting up with a different woman at the after-party when his future soul mate was in town. In town *and* going out with someone else.

No, if Raymond really wanted Julie, he would be marching his happy ass right down the Pacific Coast Highway straight to the place his woman was at and breaking up any would-be romantic notions that this wannabe playa Carlos had gotten into his head.

Dante stood and went to the door with purposeful strides. If she were his woman, that's exactly what he would do.

Chapter 7

Carlos asking her out, after they'd only had a brief conversation at the party, was completely unexpected. With Raymond busy for the night, she had no real reason not to accept his date. When Carlos mentioned visiting Sunsetters, a new restaurant and bar overlooking the ocean rumored to have the best seafood in the area, she'd readily accepted.

After devouring the delicious shrimp tortellini, Julie and Carlos ordered the gianduja chocolate soufflé to share for dessert, and Julie finished her pineapple mojito while they waited. The sun set over the ocean, bathing the late evening in oranges and reds, while a warm breeze caressed them in the outdoor seating area. The relaxing sounds of the waves hitting below the bar blended in with the lively conversation of the crowd.

The buzz from inside the restaurant increased. Carlos stopped talking, and they both glanced to the door.

"What's going on?" She lifted her head to try to see through the crowd to the excitement but couldn't see who or what it was.

"Since opening there have been several celebrities who've popped in. They always like to try the new places."

Julie nodded. "More than likely." She glanced at Carlos. "I guess our service will go down now."

He fiddled with a button on his white golf shirt—something she'd realized was a nervous habit of his. "That's not necessarily a bad thing. The longer we sit here, the more time I get to spend enjoying your company."

Carlos blatantly admired her neck and shoulders, exposed by the turquoise halter top she wore, before lowering his hand to hers on the table. He was attractive, and Julie was enjoying herself, but his hand on hers didn't ignite any of the sparks the same touch had when Dante did it.

Carlos was subtle, but his intentions were clear. He'd be willing to take their date as far as she'd let him. So far she was only willing to go as far as a good-night kiss.

"It has been a fun night."

The buzz from inside the restaurant came out onto the deck. Julie turned just as the crowd parted and a hostess ushered Dante toward the bar. She'd spent a lot of time with him this week interviewing contractors, so she really shouldn't feel so breathless to see him again. That didn't stop the air from rushing from her lungs when his dark eyes met hers from beneath the rim of his black fedora. His clothes were casual, red shorts that brushed the knee and a black button-up shirt. A diamond earring sparkled in his ear, and the glint of a platinum chain, tasteful, not big and bulky like other artists wore, peeked from his open collar.

Dante stopped following the hostess and strolled over to their table.

"Julie, funny finding you here," he said. Then he glanced at Carlos. "With Carlos."

Julie raised her chin. He didn't sound like he was surprised to see her there at all.

Carlos held out his hand. "Good to see you again."

"Same here," Dante said. Again, the tone of his voice didn't jibe with his words. She got the distinct impression that Dante didn't think seeing Carlos again was good. "I thought you were heading to the East Coast for a gig."

Carlos shook his head. "The gig fell through. Though I normally hate losing a job, losing this one opens the door to other possibilities," he said with a warm smile at Julie.

Julie returned his smile, but the movement felt brittle. She drummed her fingers on the table, suddenly annoyed about Dante being there. She had been enjoying her time with Carlos and the slight attraction she felt toward him. Then *he* had to walk in and, with just a look, turn her insides as soft and gooey as the soufflé she'd ordered—a look, a smile and way too much sex appeal to be fair.

"What brings you here?" she asked.

Dante leaned his hand on the back of her side of the booth. The breeze chose that second to conspire against her and wrapped her in the masculine scent of his cologne. "I was hoping to run into someone. A person I'd like to spend a lot more time with, but she keeps avoiding being alone with me."

Intense dark eyes zeroed in on her, and the melodic tenor of his voice sang to her soul. *You'll initiate the kiss.* Words spoken with the confidence of a man who had years of experience with women not hesitating to be alone with him after only knowing him a week. She wanted to kiss him. Thought about kissing him several times while they interviewed contractors, which is why she'd clung to her rule to never show a guy how much he rattled her. If she gave Dante the upper hand, he'd have her mind twisted in knots over him in less than an hour.

"I hope the person you're looking for shows up," she said.

"She already has," he said. "Enjoy your date, but call me later." The sentence wasn't a question. It was a clear and definite command. Cocking a brow, Dante nodded to Carlos and then casually strolled back to the hostess, who took him to the bar.

Julie's mouth fell open. Had he just tried to stake a claim on her in the middle of her date? She had no quick comeback—a first for her. She had rules and maneuvers for the sly games men played. Straightforward and blatant moves of possession weren't something she was used to.

"I guess I have some competition for your affections," Carlos said in a good-natured tone, but his fingers toyed with the button of his shirt.

Julie snapped her mouth shut and looked away from Dante. "I'm sorry, what?"

Carlos gave a knowing smile. "Dante is interested in you."

She pulled her thoughts together and sat up straighter. "Interested or not, I don't date business partners. He's just being persistent because I made that rule very clear. He's only interested because I'm not falling at his feet. Men like him enjoy the chase, but the chase is all they're interested in."

"You make attraction sound so matter-of-fact. You don't think he'd want you if you made his pursuit easier?"

She shrugged. "I doubt it. Most women would die to be with Dante Wilson, whether or not falling for him was considered unprofessional. I'm one of the rare women who won't—therefore, he's interested. That's the way guys are. They're intrigued by women who are different. We women get sucked into the thrill of being chased and let our guards down, only to have the guy grow tired of the novelty after he's gotten to know you better. Then we're left in love and heartbroken, while he moves on to once again chase someone else. It's a cruel but never-ending cycle."

Carlos flinched, then took a sip of his drink. "Ouch, you have a bitter view of our sex."

This wasn't the first time a man had called her bitter, and the claim didn't bother Julie. When faced with the truth, most guys preferred attributing the truth to a woman's bitterness. "I'm not bitter, just realistic."

He leaned on the table and took her hand between his. "And what's my interest in you?"

"I think you are attracted to me and want to start a casual dating thing while I'm in town."

His grin would be considered dangerous to her heart, if Dante hadn't already threatened it. "Oh, really?"

"Really, with the ultimate goal of getting me into bed. I'm going to let you know now that I'm very selective about the men I sleep with, so don't get your hopes up."

"Double ouch," Carlos said, but his grin remained. "You are different."

Julie shrugged. "Aren't we all?"

Laughter came from the bar. Julie glanced that way to the small crowd of people who now surrounded Dante. Carlos squeezed her hand, and she tore her gaze away from Dante.

"I like *your* different."

The waiter returned with their dessert, and she quickly pulled away from Carlos's grasp. She didn't like what she saw in his eyes. Desire, genuine interest, but also some type of calculation. He was probably choosing the best tactic to get her into bed. She liked Carlos all right, but she wouldn't play with his emotions by pretending like she wanted to take him to bed. She could practically hear Evette sucking her teeth before saying, "See, there you go pushing a good man away again." Maybe she was, but the truth was she was only in California until the club opened. After that, she had no interest in pursuing a long-term relationship.

They ate the delicious soufflé, and Carlos made her laugh with his interesting stories about working with various recording artists. As much as she tried to focus on the rest of her date, her attention kept diverting to Dante. And while he gave a good show of enjoying the crowd of people hanging on to his every word, she caught several of the glances he threw her way. To make things worse, every time she was distracted, noticing Dante notice her, Carlos noticed them both pretending not to look at the other.

Dante stayed for only thirty minutes, long enough to order a drink, take a few pictures with fans and delight the crowd. He paid his tab and left, a smug smirk on his face as he waved goodbye to her and Carlos. The smugness annoyed her more than him showing up. Of course, he would know his arrival would distract her from her date. He was throwing her off her game, and she didn't like it.

The interest in Carlos's eyes had slowly morphed into defeat with every glance she'd tried to sneak Dante's way. Julie checked the time, ready to end the ruined date. "I really should get back now. I've got a long day ahead."

Carlos nodded and signaled for the waiter. "You can bring the check now."

The waiter shook his head and smiled. "No need. Dante took care of it already, along with the tip. You two have a good night."

Julie's jaw dropped. Carlos tried to grin, but the smile was flat. "I guess Dante just upped the ante."

Julie snapped her mouth shut and gritted her teeth. "I'm so sorry, Carlos. That was uncalled for."

He shrugged. "Hey, he's a man used to getting what he wants. Looks like he really wants you."

His attempt to sound unbothered was ruined by the annoyance in his voice. She couldn't blame him; there wasn't a man she knew who would accept another guy swooping in and covering the costs of his date. Dante's my-cock's-bigger-than-yours move was bold and un-called for.

Go hard or go home.

Julie fumed as they left the restaurant. Dante may not want to accept that she was serious about nothing happening between them, but that wasn't her problem. He was just another smug, arrogant celebrity who thought he could buy anything he wanted, including her affections. Well, the man had better get his mind right. She would make absolutely sure he understood that you didn't play games with Julie Dominick.

Julie swerved the rental car to the gate blocking the way to Dante's house. She wanted to plow right through the wrought iron blockage, drive straight to the front of his house and bang on his door. Instead she lowered the driver's window and smashed the button on the call box with her finger.

"Hello, Julie." His sexy tenor filtered through the machine.

Damn him and her body for the tremble that went through her. "How did you know I was calling?"

"Smile for the camera."

Julie glared at the box, then the security camera affixed to the top of the gate.

"Did you come by to thank me for dinner?"

Trembles forgotten, anger shot through her. "Not at all. We need to talk."

"Come on in," he said. A buzzing sound filled the air before the gate opened.

Julie gritted her teeth and entered the property. The sun had set, but the view of his home in the dark was just as spectacular as during the day. Lights led the way down the long drive, nestled in tropical plants. More lights shone directly onto the stone villa, giving the place a warm and welcoming feel. The beauty of the place nearly took her breath away. Nearly. She was still too angry to appreciate his wealth. After jumping out of the car, she slammed the door and marched to the large wooden door.

Before she could bang out her anger with her fist, it swung open. He'd changed into loose black lounging pants, which flowed around his long legs in dark waves. A sleeveless white T-shirt clung to every muscle of his torso. Julie licked her lips and fought to breathe normally. He seemed to constantly snatch the air from her lungs.

"Hello, Julie," he said again, stepping back and holding the door open.

"You've got some nerve, Dante." She didn't cross the threshold. Wouldn't go into the house. Couldn't, when he looked like he was ready to jump into bed, and everything from his eyes, scent and smile invited her to jump in with him.

"Really? Why?"

"How dare you pay for dinner?"

"I dare because I wanted to."

"What would make you want to do something so smug, arrogant and rude? You should have seen the look on Carlos's face."

He smirked and shrugged before leaning against the door. "I almost stuck around just so I could see the look on his face."

Julie crossed her arms beneath her breasts and glared. "You think this is funny?"

"Imagining the look on his face?" His full sensual lips lifted with humor as he nodded. "Yeah, kind of."

"Well, it wasn't funny. You had no right to do that. We were on a date."

"I know."

"If you knew that, then why would you pay for our dinner? Didn't you think about how it would make Carlos feel to have another guy pay for his date's meal?"

Dante stood straight. He placed a hand on the doorjamb and leaned in close. "I didn't give a damn and still don't care what Carlos thinks or feels. You should have been there with me. Not him."

If she were a violent person, she would have slapped the smirk right off his handsome face. "I'm not going out with you. I don't want to go out with you."

Dante grinned. "Yes, you do." He turned and strolled into the house.

"Where are you going?" she shouted after his retreating back.

He looked over his shoulder. "Inside." He continued walking.

"I don't want to come inside. I don't want to be here at all."

He spun around but didn't come back to the door. "Yes, you do. If you didn't want to be here, you and Carlos would've been thankful to enjoy a nice meal on my dime. He would have taken you back to your hotel, where, after an awkward 'can I come in for coffee' conversation, you would have either sent him home or invited him inside. Based on the looks you threw my way over dinner, I think you would've sent him home. But on the off chance that you did invite him in, you would have forgotten any indignation over my paying for the meal and had a mediocre first-date kiss. Instead you dropped him and rushed to see me." He rested his hands on his chest. "Why? To pretend as if you're angry? When you're really here because you wanted to see me."

Julie scoffed. "You're conceited and delusional."

"Conceited, yes, delusional, no. Now quit hiding behind your excuse that you can't mix business and pleasure or some trumped-up anger over me making sure Carlos has no doubt that he's got some serious competition."

Julie's body went rigid. She stomped over the threshold and was in his face a second later. "Let's get a few things straight. The reason Carlos and I didn't have the 'come in for coffee conversation' is because I don't invite a guy up on the first date. If he makes it to three or more, then we'll see. For your information, our first kiss was hardly mediocre despite your attempt to butt in on the night."

A dark scowl replaced his smug look. While her good-night kiss with Carlos was nothing more than a quick peck and a hug, it had been nice enough to describe as more than mediocre, especially to get the triumphant gleam out of Dante's eyes.

"As for me hiding behind an excuse that I can't mix business and pleasure—" she took a step closer, leaning her head back to stare into his eyes "—it's not because I can't. It's because I don't. Proving that I deserve the jobs I get is hard enough without adding assumptions that I'm only successful because I sleep with womanizers like you in order to land projects. So, whether or not you've decided to be *serious competition* with Carlos or not, just remember I'm not some helpless rabbit you can lure into a trap. I've avoided wolves much deadlier than you. You won't catch me unless I want to get caught."

She slid her foot back to step away. His hand shot out and latched on to her waist. Dante closed the scant distance between them and pressed his solid body against hers. "Don't stand so close if you don't want to get caught."

Desire coated every nuance of his voice. The air around them shifted, crackling and sparking with the anger, annoyance and attraction simmering between them. The line between anger and desire was thin, and when his long fingers flexed against her waist, the line snapped. He infuriated her. The audacity of him paying for the meal, declaring himself competition, insisting that being zapped by the electric current between them was inevitable. Yet she couldn't listen to the faint voice that said to pull away. Sucking in a breath, she didn't smell cologne. The clean smell of masculine soap and the intoxicating heat of his body made her mouth water. Her nipples tightened. Heat settled heavily between her thighs.

"Now that I've got you," he said, his tenor lowering to a seductive bass, "what are you going to do?"

Julie swallowed. "Depends on what your intentions are."

"I intend to get the truth out of you." His hand, strong and sure, slid from her waist to her back. She didn't think he could pull her closer, but he did, and the rock-hard proof of his arousal grew between them.

She wanted to turn, walk away and call him a fool. She licked her lips, and slowly drew the lower one between her teeth. His eyes heated, and his lids lowered. She wanted to kiss him more.

Embracing his face with her hands, Julie pulled him down to do just that. Briefly she realized he'd proved her a liar—she'd initiated the kiss. A second later, the pleasure of his lips against hers blew away all other thought. A low groan rumbled through his chest, and his strong arms wrapped around her midsection, squeezing her tight. His tongue traced her lower lip, and she quickly opened her mouth, gliding hers over his in slow, erotic strokes. One of her arms wrapped around his neck; her other hand brushed the stubble on his strong jaw.

The heat between her legs ached for release. Her heart pumped against her ribs. She imagined peeling his clothes off and dragging him up the stairs. She imagined kissing every inch of his perfect body and spending the night moaning his name in ecstasy or having him right here, hot and fast, in the foyer fully clothed. The how and the why didn't matter as long as Dante was pressed hard and deep inside her.

Never had her body yearned for a man as much as it did right now. A yearning so strong that she didn't care about anything other than his lean hips between her legs, which could lead to rash decisions that would hurt her and her career, and add fuel to the rumors of her success.

She broke the kiss but didn't jump out of his arms. A moment later, Dante's eyes opened slowly, the dark irises dazed and burning with the same longing chewing on her insides. She wanted him but not tonight, not when she was going on need alone. Her rule was to never sleep with a guy unless she fully understood what she was getting into, even more so, when sleeping with a guy like Dante could hinder, not help, her reputation. The club opening successfully was the most important thing.

Dante's nostrils flared with heavy breaths, and he watched her with deep, hungry eyes. Her body shuddered. She had to get out of there before she said screw it and screwed him.

"Now that you've caught me," she said, hoping he didn't notice the needy trembling of her voice, "how will you keep me?"

His brows drew together. She lifted on her toes and pressed a kiss to the side of his lips. "Good night, Dante."

Pulling out of his inviting arms was torture. Every agonizing brush of her skin against his as she did so made her want to wrap her arms around him, kiss him again, taste his skin and feel his body on hers.

Not tonight. Not without thinking about this and being sure. Use your head, not your heart.

He let her go and looked just as dazed as she felt. She walked to the door with what she hoped was a confident stroll that masked her wobbly knees. If he guessed how difficult walking away from him was for her and pulled her back into his arms, she'd say to hell with thinking this thing through and drag Dante upstairs directly to his bedroom.

Chapter 8

Dante's ringing cell phone interrupted his repeated attempts to work on the song he was writing for S.A.F. Normally, when he was in his music studio, surrounded by the various instruments his parents insisted he learn to play and gazing at the platinum and gold records hanging on the walls, inspiration struck. But today wasn't a normal day. He'd kissed Julie the day before. No, Julie had kissed the hell out of him, then walked away.

He picked up his cell phone from the corner of the upright piano. He usually didn't bring the phone in here with him, but he'd expected a phone call from his sexy developer. Raymond's number was on the screen.

Swallowing disappointment, Dante answered. "Raymond, what's up?"

"Man, you missed one hell of an after-party last night. What happened?"

Dante could taste Julie's sweet lips and nearly groaned. "Something came up."

Raymond laughed. "I bet it did. Hey, are you busy?"

"Working on a new song." Or he would be if his brain would stop reliving the memory of Julie's curves pressed against him.

"Is this for the solo album you're putting out? Your own music?"

"Not for me but for S.A.F. I'm meeting with them at the studio later today."

The reason Dante chose Malibu for his nightclub instead of LA was the small following S.A.F. already had in the area. Launching S.A.F. in their hometown was the best way to ensure they came out of the gate strong.

"If you're writing the music, then I know it's going to be hot. Look, I called to ask a favor."

"What kind of favor?"

"Nothing big. Since you've already helped Julie pick the contractor, can you handle overseeing the rest of the opening for the next few weeks?"

Dante frowned and put down the pencil he'd been using to erase the last few notes of music he'd put to paper. "Why? Do you want out?"

"No, I just got an offer to perform in London. It's some type of music festival, and while I'm there, my agent said I could work on being a guest judge for this talent show they've got on television. After the concert tour, this will be a good way to keep my music out there. I know I promised to help you open this place."

Dante stood and walked across the room to stand before the window. The view of the solid, long-lasting profile of the mountains from this side of the house inspired him more than the changing tides of the ocean did.

"I understand. You're still building your career. I'd be going, too, if I were in your position. Besides, you've already helped out by recommending Julie. She seems to know what she's doing."

Both with the club and with keeping him guessing. He still couldn't believe she'd walked away without a backward glance. Were his skills slipping? Any other woman would have dragged him upstairs after a kiss like that.

"I told you she would. Julie is the other part of the favor. I hate leaving her out here. I know I just asked you to keep your distance, but do you mind showing her a good time while I'm gone?"

Would he mind? Dante almost laughed at the idea that he would have a problem spending more time with Julie. "The question is will *you* mind?"

"I told you how I felt about Julie, and I trust you."

A microscopic sliver of guilt whispered in Dante's head for the barest of seconds. Along with the idea that maybe he should confess to Raymond that he'd kissed Julie the night before and planned to kiss her a lot more before this project was finished. Even in those barest of seconds, he knew he wouldn't. Dante couldn't shake the feeling that if Raymond really wanted a future with Julie, he'd be paying a lot more attention to her now.

"Have you talked to Julie yet? Maybe Carlos and her hit things off, and she wants you out of town."

"I called her before calling you to let her know. She was upset that I wasn't going to be here but said she understood. Plus, I'm not worried about Carlos. She said the date was fun but that she didn't think they'd be going out again."

Dante grinned and leaned against the windowsill. "She give a reason why?"

"She was vague about why, but that's Julie. She doesn't need a good reason to drop a guy. That's why I know she's waiting for me."

Dante grunted and shook his head, thankful that Raymond wouldn't see his disbelieving expression. "I'll invite her to some parties while she's here, introduce her to some people."

"Cool. I'll call and check on progress when I can."

Dante could hear the goodbye coming, but he spoke up quickly. "You going alone?"

"I'm taking the singer from the club last night. We had a good time, and I'd like to keep it going."

With that, the sliver of guilt vanished completely. "You do that."

They said goodbye, then got off the phone. Dante checked his watch and swore. His choreographer was coming over in an hour, and he'd wasted the entire morning daydreaming about Julie. He couldn't remember ever doing that, not even in his teens. He'd had women throwing themselves at him like rice at a wedding since he had hit puberty.

Dante did an internal calculation of how long he'd practice the new routine for his next music video. If he cut the session back an hour, he'd have time to get to the studio an hour earlier. Hopefully, it would give him just enough time to set up a late dinner with Julie and see for himself just how "upset" she was about Raymond leaving. He would pull out all the stops to impress her tonight. He was Dante Wilson, and women loved him. He was sure that after tonight, if there were any lingering embers smoldering from their kiss, he was going to set them on fire.

"So how are things going in sunny California?" Evette's excited voice came through Julie's cell phone.

Julie sat back in the chair at the desk in her hotel suite. "Things are going great. They agreed to bring Dominant Development on as a full partner."

"As if there was any doubt."

No need to mention that she didn't give Dante and Raymond much of a choice. She'd come in as if she already had the job. Luckily, Dante was impressed with the contractors she'd chosen.

"Today I'm meeting with the city to make sure I know everything they'll need when I apply for permits. I know we're good zoning-wise, but I'm not sure about what we'll need for the building renovations."

"Is Sheila coming to the meeting?" Evette asked, referring to the contractor they'd hired. Dante had insisted on hiring Sheila over Orlando. They both had good reputations, but Julie was a little concerned with the way Sheila avoided sharing how she always came in under budget on her projects. Julie called her references, and no one had anything bad to say about Sheila's work, so Julie pushed aside her concerns and went with Dante's decision.

"Yep, she's dealt with the people at the city before and knows what they'll ask for. Dante already has an architect handling the redesign of the building, so he's coming, as well. I have no fears things won't go as planned."

"Or as close to plans. Wait until construction starts— that's when things get dicey."

Julie nodded. "Ain't that the truth."

"So how are other things?" Evette's voice was filled with expectancy.

"Things like what?"

"Oh, come on. Every time we talk it's only about work, I can't stand it anymore. Tell me about Dante. What's he like? Is he as sexy in person as he looks on television? What about his voice? Is it as smooth as it sounds on his songs? Does he smell good?"

Julie chuckled. "Smell good?"

"Yes, you can tell a lot about a man by the way he smells."

If Julie went by smell alone, Dante was delicious, filling and addictive. If she were describing food using those words she'd know she would need to be careful about overindulging. After last night's kiss, Julie was on the verge of binging on her craving for Dante.

"He smells all right, I guess. He is nice and eager to get the club opened. He helped pick Sheila."

"He's not one of those micromanagers, is he? Sticking his nose in every aspect of the project?"

"I don't think so. He let me ask most of the questions and handle the meetings. He only chimed in when he needed clarification. I think we'll be okay."

"Good, but I do hope you'll get to have some fun while you're there."

"I'm here for a job. Not to have fun." *Or an affair with a superstar.* "How are things back home?"

They chatted about the two projects they'd started before Julie came to California, and Evette's success with interviewing some new people. After promising to send Julie the names and interview notes before the end of the day, they got off the phone. Julie glanced at her watch; she had two hours until the meeting with the city. She jumped up from the desk and pulled the belt of her silver satin robe tight. She'd already picked out the suit she would wear today and showered before working. All that was left was to eat something quick, dress and get down to city hall.

Someone knocked on the door just as she picked up the phone to order from room service. She pulled the robe tighter and went to the door. She glanced through the peephole and saw Dante. Tiny pinpricks of heat spread up her chest, neck and cheeks. Really—she was blushing, and he couldn't even see her.

The night before she'd considered everything that would have happened if she hadn't walked away, contemplated all the outcomes that could result if she slept with him and concluded that keeping their relationship professional was for the best.

Taking a deep breath, she opened the door. "Can I help you?"

Dante's gaze traveled from the tips of her manicured toes up to her face, so hot and thorough that she might as well have left the robe on the floor. She stood cement still with her arms crossed over her breasts and her chin lifted, hiding how much his gaze affected her, when she really wanted to squirm under his appreciative appraisal.

"Go out with me tonight?"

The request to go out with him wasn't unexpected. She had kissed him pretty thoroughly the night before. A date would give her the chance to talk with him about the project more. All his expected and unoriginal attempts to get her to sleep with him would annoy her enough that finding reasons to stay out of his bed would be easier.

"Where?"

Dante stepped forward and placed his hand on the door. "At this sushi place I like. We'll have time to talk."

"What do we need to discuss?"

"The kiss last night. My plans to keep you now that I've caught you."

The words stirred up the desire she was trying to suppress. She took a step back but couldn't escape the heat of his body or how great he smelled. "I took you for a catch-and-throw type of guy, especially since I'm only in town for a short while."

"You're in town long enough." He reached forward and took one of the ends of the belt that held her robe closed in his hand. His fingers slid across the silky material. "I'm fine with holding on to you while you're here."

He didn't pull on the material, but she was suddenly very aware that she was nearly naked beneath the robe. A simple tug would loosen the knot and the sides would fall open, exposing Dante to her in nothing but a lacy sky blue bra and matching panties. Would he trace the edges of the lace with his fingertips? Would his hands slide across her naked waist to pull her against his firm body? Her breasts felt heavy, and her nipples tightened to sensitive points. The shots of heat beneath her skin took aim and fired at the junction between her thighs.

Think about what he said, Julie. "I'm fine with holding on to you while you're here." He'd already put her in the quick-and-easy-sex category. She didn't do the quick-

and-easy-sex thing, especially with men she worked with. She couldn't afford to get caught up in him.

"About that kiss. I was angr—"

His hand snaked around her waist. He pulled her against him and dropped his head to kiss her, taking full advantage of the fact that she was midsentence and that her lips were already parted. All her considerations, contemplations and conclusions crashed into a pile at her feet. Soft, feminine moans surrounded them, and Julie accepted that the man had her purring like a kitten in less than a second. He kissed her softly and thoroughly, her body sliding against his thanks to the slippery material of her robe. Her hands clenched his strong arms, and she shifted her torso just enough that the aching peaks of her breasts brushed his chest. Dante's hands tightened on her waist, his hips pressed forward until the length of his desire pushed against her midsection.

He lifted his head. "Don't say no yet." There was a sexy, confident lift to his full lips, but underneath the swagger, she heard the plea. He really wanted her to say yes. Long fingers flexed on her lower back, and he took in her cleavage, revealed by the gaping opening of her robe. "I'll pick you up at nine."

Refusing to go on one date now seemed juvenile and fearful. She wasn't afraid of Dante—afraid of her body's reaction maybe, but not of him. "Nine it is."

He lowered his head, but Julie quickly stepped out of his reach. He smirked and raised a brow but didn't push. "I'll see you tonight." He softly hit the inside of the door with the side of his hand, then turned and left.

Julie shut the door and leaned heavily against the cool wood. She'd definitely lost this round. Big-time.

She knew the rules to the game he was playing. Dante wanted to conquer the walls protecting her panties, not her heart. She was here to do a job, strengthen her business and not add to the rumors trying to cling to her reputation. She'd best remember that and get her head back on what was best for her long-term, not consider a short-term affair with a man who, without purpose, could divide and conquer both walls.

Chapter 9

As much as Dante looked forward to going out with Julie that night, he had to drag himself away from the studio with S.A.F. They'd made good progress putting music to the song he'd written and then started working on other music. If his date was with any other woman he would have canceled, but the memory of Julie in that sexy silver robe and the sweet sounds she'd made when he kissed her had him throwing up deuces to the guys in just enough time so he wouldn't be late picking her up.

When she met him in her hotel's lobby, he wished he'd left the studio earlier. She wore a sleeveless cream jumpsuit. The low V in the front provided a teasing glimpse of her cleavage, and the loose pants draped nicely over her curves. A gold belt cinched her waist, and red heels gave her height. For a second, he could do nothing but stare. Her amber eyes sparkled, and her sensual lips rose in a smile that made his cock twitch and his chest swell.

"You look beautiful," he said when she reached him.

"Thank you. You don't look half bad yourself."

He ran a hand down the front of his outfit: white jacket, black dress shirt, fitted black pants, set off by a black-and-white-checked handkerchief in the pocket.

"I aim to please." He held out his arm for her. She slipped her hand into the crook of his elbow and smiled at him. He felt a dead-on sensation that Julie, on his arm, going out with him, was right—like she belonged next to him and no one else.

Dante shook the thought away. Whatever happened with him and Julie would be temporary. He was no-where near ready for anything more than a few weeks of fun. Despite her passionate response to his kiss, the way she held a part of herself back told him that she was a woman looking for forever. She wasn't quick to fall, which meant he'd have to be careful when they slept together. He wanted her, but he didn't want to hurt her.

He led her out to his mocha-black Mercedes AMG CLS coupe and opened the door for her.

"I hope you like sushi," he said after getting in on his side.

"I do."

He put the car in gear and slipped into traffic to-ward Arata, the sushi bar and restaurant named after the Japanese chef who had become a celebrity after a string of successful cooking shows. Dante had hoped to get to know her a little better on the drive, but she guided the conversation with updates on her meetings with the city that day. He was impressed by how much she'd gotten clarified concerning the permits required.

She turned toward him in her seat. "The architect you hired already has the renovation plans drawn up. It's just getting them finalized and submitted to the city for review. If all goes well, we'll have the plans submitted in a week or so, and then we just wait for the city to approve. Once that's done, construction will begin."

He briefly took his eyes off the road to glance at her. "That soon?"

"Yep."

"Dang, you are good."

She laughed. "I wish I could take all the credit, but if your architect hadn't already been on the ball, and Sheila hadn't known as much as she does about the city's permitting process, things would have taken a lot longer. I don't have all the contacts I need out here to maneuver things as quickly."

"And here I thought you were a miracle worker," he teased.

"I am, but I also know my limitations."

He pulled up to the front of the restaurant and Julie's brows rose. "Arata," Julie said. "When I called I couldn't get a reservation until a month out."

She put her hand on the door, and he stilled her with a hand on her knee. "I called up Mr. Arata himself."

She didn't seem as impressed with that as he'd expected, but she did smile. "That's nice."

"I'll get your door." He got out and waved for the valet to wait so that he could open the door for Julie.

"Welcome back, Mr. Wilson," the valet said, taking the keys from Dante. "I hope you and your date enjoy your evening."

"Thank you, Marcel," he said to the man and turned to Julie.

"You're on first-name basis with the valet," she said as they walked to the door. "Do you come here often?"

"It's one of my favorite places." His favorite first-date place because getting a reservation was so hard that most of his dates were awestruck by his ability to get them in on a moment's notice.

"I read about this place before coming out. They're supposed to have the best sushi in the area."

"Well, I'm glad that I'm able to bring you here," he said with a grin.

She clasped her hands and bounced her shoulders. He wasn't sure if her excitement was for the food or being with him; either way, he was doing well so far. They entered the restaurant, and the hostess, Mika, looked up at them. *Ah, damn, I forgot about her.* He'd slept with Mika right before the concert tour. Her dark eyes widened, and a sexy grin crossed her face.

"Dante, it's so good to see you again," Mika said in a low and sensual voice. "I wondered how long it would be before you came in now that your tour is over."

Dante chuckled uneasily. "Mika, I didn't know you worked on Fridays."

She shrugged. "When I heard we had a special guest coming tonight, I agreed to help out. We've got your table ready."

Julie looked up at Dante with a cocked brow. "Your table?"

"One of my favorite spots," he said.

Mika moved around the hostess stand. She wore the same tight black dress and obscenely high heels that made him invite her to his house for the party before the tour. "And we love that you come here," Mika purred. "All of us." Her voice dripped with meaning.

Julie looked between them, and understanding flashed in her amber eyes. He swallowed a groan. He'd had fun with a few of the waitresses there, as well. There weren't many hostesses or waitresses in this town that he hadn't invited to a party, bought a drink for or flirted with. Maybe he should have driven her to LA instead. More restaurants to choose from with a smaller likelihood he'd dallied with the beautiful waitstaff.

"All of them," Julie said with that knowing smile of hers.

He tried to shrug off Mika's comment. "I tip well."

"Yeah, I'm sure."

They followed Mika to his table in the back, sheltered from view of the other patrons and next to floor-to-ceiling windows that provided a perfect romantic view of the ocean. He waved at a few other celebrities, politicians and businesspeople he recognized. Instead of being impressed by his contacts, Julie's knowing grin only grew as a few waitresses stopped what they were doing to greet him with blushing cheeks and inviting smiles.

"You must tip very well," Julie said once they were seated. "The waitresses love you."

"Overly warm greetings come with the territory of being a celebrity."

"Yeah, sure," she said with a twinkle in her eye before looking at the menu.

"Good evening, Dante," a woman said.

Dante looked up at their waitress and cringed. "Hello, Katie." Of course he'd get Katie.

"I'll be serving you tonight. Don't hesitate to let me know if you need…anything." Her lips curved up seductively.

Julie looked up from the menu and shot a questioning glance at Katie. Dante shifted in his seat and pretended he hadn't heard the invitation in Katie's voice. He once again second-guessed himself for bringing Julie here. Historically for him, when other women showed interest, the woman he was currently with clung harder. He should have realized that when confronted with his conquests, Julie would pull away.

"Thank you, Katie. We'd like a bottle of—"

"The Fallen Angel sake?" Katie finished. "I've already instructed the bar for you. Would you also like to start with the lobster seviche?"

Julie chuckled and studied her menu. Dante nodded at Katie. "That will be fine."

Were his moves that apparent, that predictable? Well, it wasn't as if he had to try very hard to be imaginative. Most of the time, asking the woman out was enough; bringing her here was just part of the pizzazz of going out with Dante Wilson.

Do you realize how shallow that sounds?

He pushed the thought aside along with the shake in confidence that being Dante Wilson wasn't enough to impress Julie. He hadn't had to try to impress a woman…ever.

Katie made a move to turn. "You know what," Julie said, stopping her. "I'd like to start with the sashimi salad. I don't particularly care for seviche."

She gave Katie a tight smile, then looked back at her menu.

"Oh," Katie said. "Of course. I'll be right back with that."

Dante looked to Julie and decided changing the subject was best. "Are you enjoying your time in Malibu so far?"

She didn't look up from the menu. "Tell me, Dante—have you slept with every woman in this restaurant or just the hostess and our waitress?"

"Excuse me?"

"I think the question was pretty clear."

"You know what—they don't matter." He reached across the table and pulled her menu away. He took her hands in his. "All that matters is being here with you tonight. I don't want to spend my evening with anyone else."

Some of the skepticism in her eyes diminished, but she still pulled her hands away and rested them in her lap. Damn, he needed to get this date back on track. His cell phone chimed in his pocket.

Julie glanced around. "Did you hear that?"

"Just my cell. That's the sound when I get a text. I'll ignore. I'm more interested in learning more about you."

"Okay, what would you like to know?"

"What made you start your business?" His cell chimed again.

She lifted her brows as if asking if he was going to look, but he ignored it again.

"I couldn't work for Nexon-Jones anymore."

Dante leaned back and regarded her. Nexon-Jones was *the* name in nightclub development. His family worked with them, and he knew the salaries of their top people were well over six figures. "Why not? They've got a great reputation."

"I *was* moving up in the business and could have easily seen myself being there forever. I loved it."

"What happened?"

"We were on the line to open a club in Las Vegas. I really wanted to manage the project because everyone knew that whoever handled the opening of the Vegas club was a shoo-in for a new venue in Japan. My boss approached me about doing a job in New York, and when I brought up the Vegas club, he said he wanted me specifically on the New York club and that landing it was crucial. If I did, I'd be in charge of the Japanese club."

"That doesn't sound like a reason to leave."

"I could only secure the project because the property owner indicated that he'd like to spend some *private* time with me before deciding to sell."

Dante's hand clenched into a fist. "He wanted you to sleep with the owner just to get the property?"

"Pretty much. When I went to HR, they didn't believe me. Neither did his partner, or at least they said they didn't believe me. I think the man just controls the HR department. So I left and took Evette with me. She's my business partner."

There wasn't a hint of bitterness in her voice; he imagined that walking away from such a successful career had to have been difficult. "That takes guts."

"Starting my own business?"

"No, going to human resources. I'm familiar with Nexon-Jones, and I know the culture. It's a definite boys' club. To take your accusations to HR was brave, doing so means the next woman he tries that with will have the history of your accusation to stand on."

"I hope so. I knew nothing would really happen, but if he did that to me, then he'd do it to someone else." Dante's phone chimed again. Julie glanced toward his jacket pocket. "You probably need to check that."

He agreed and pulled out his phone. There were several messages from the guys in S.A.F. They were still in the studio working on the music they'd started, and apparently they were having a major breakthrough on some new music.

"Damn."

"Something wrong?" Julie asked.

He looked up from his phone. "No. Not really. I was in the studio before coming here, and the group I'm working with, the ones I want to headline at the club when it's open, are still there. They've got a new track they want me to hear."

Katie came back with the sake, appetizer and Julie's salad. She grinned at Dante. "Are you ready for me to serve you?"

"Actually, can you give us another minute?" he said shortly.

Katie blinked rapidly, looked between him and Julie, then nodded. "Um, sure, whatever you want."

When she walked away, he looked over at Julie, then glanced around at the restaurant. It was only popular because a celebrity chef owned it, and celebrities like Dante frequented the place to see and be seen. Everything about it was created to impress. The long waiting list, beautiful waitresses and overpriced food that barely covered the plate. All for show but showing nothing, not good enough to really impress Julie. She'd walked away from a position that would have taken her far in order to preserve her values. Despite the sparks between them, she would easily walk away from him for the same reasons.

He met her eye. "You want to get out of here?"

She dropped the menu and nodded. "Yes."

"Good, because I have someplace I'd like to show you."

Chapter 10

Julie expected Dante to take her back to his place or some other fancy location that he would try to astound her with, so when he pulled up in front of an old two-story brick building, she gave him a questioning look.

"What's this?" she asked.

"It's where I make my kind of music." He got out of the car and jogged around to let her out.

"It looks abandoned."

"The first floor is. The second holds a studio."

He grasped her hand, his grip warm and steady, then eagerly led her inside. There was a small open foyer that may have once been a reception area. The dim lights and the lack of a chair or computer behind the dusty desk made her doubt that the foyer was still used. They crossed the scratched wooden floors to an elevator. The wheels creaked and groaned after Dante pressed the up button.

"You make music here?"

"Yep." That was all she got before he ushered her onto the elevator and pressed the second button. The sounds of creaking and groaning seemed much more ominous when she was actually inside the elevator. When the doors opened again, the muffled sound of music greeted them.

The lights were on, but it was still not brilliantly bright. He led her past a few offices on the left and stopped before a door on the right—the source of the music. Dante opened the door to what Julie could see was a music studio. One guy sat in the control room, where she and Dante had entered. Behind the glass, two men played a melodic and upbeat song on violins, another was on drums and a fourth stood behind a turntable playing what sounded like hip-hop that blended with the violins and drums.

The guy at the controls turned and grinned when he saw Dante. He clicked something and spoke into a microphone.

"Guys, Dante's back." The music stopped, and they all turned to Dante.

"Dante, you came back," one of the violinists said after they filed into the control room. He had dark brown skin, a faded haircut and stylish dark glasses framed beautiful hazel eyes.

"You guys said you were making good music," Dante said. "I thought I'd come and show Julie what I do in my spare time."

All eyes zeroed in on Julie. The musicians all appeared relaxed and comfortable in jeans and T-shirts. She felt overdressed and very on the spot in her jumpsuit. She lifted one hand and waved.

"Hey."

The other violinist, with the same brown skin and eyes but no glasses and a wild curly afro, put down his instrument and held out his hand.

He smiled, revealing even white teeth. "Hello, Julie," he said.

Dante wrapped a hand around her shoulder. "Guys, this is Julie Dominick. The developer extraordinaire overseeing the opening of my new club. Julie, this is Terrance." He indicated the man who'd come over and shaken her hand. "Tommy." He pointed to the other guy with the glasses. "They are the lead musicians for S.A.F., short for Strings A Flame. This is the rest of the group. Joey." The drummer raised his hand. "Lem." The guy on the turntable gave her a head nod. "And Bobby." He indicated the man who handled the controls.

"It's nice to meet all of you," she said. "S.A.F.—are you a new group?"

Terrance shook his head. "We've been playing together for five years and do shows locally. Dante is trying to take us mainstream."

She glanced at Dante. "Really?"

"Well, since they won't officially let me be a member, I have to promise fame and fortune for them to let me play with them."

She laughed along with the rest of the group.

"Seriously, this is who I've been telling you about. They'll be the entertainment act at my club. I'm introducing them to my fans, and at the same time, I plan to release my first album with them. My own music," he said with excitement in his voice.

"Your music? I'm pretty sure I've listened to your music since I was fourteen."

His arm around her shoulder tightened for a second. "You've heard the mainstream music that my family specializes in. This is what I hear when I'm writing music. Come on, guys—let's show Julie what I'm talking about."

He pointed to a beat-up old leather couch along the wall, and Julie walked over and sat. Dante slapped Bobby on the shoulder before going into the studio. "Let's start with the song we worked on earlier. Then we can get into the music you all put together after I left."

Julie sat on the edge of the couch and watched. After the first few bars, she knew she loved the music. Tommy and Terrance played a catchy melody while Dante accompanied them on the piano. Lem added a bass beat that Joey complemented with the drums. Before long, Julie was nodding her head and swaying. It was a fusion of classical, jazz and hip-hop.

When they finished, Dante glanced at her over the top of the piano. His gaze darted from her to the piano. Was he nervous?

She clapped. "That was fantastic. I've never heard that before."

Dante's shoulders relaxed. He finally met her gaze with pride and excitement in his eyes. He had been anxious about her response.

Terrance drummed his fingers on the back of his violin. "Wait until you hear this. Dante, listen to what we came up with and tell us what you think. We're missing something."

Terrance positioned the violin beneath his chin and

counted out the beat. The rest of the group started an upbeat song punctuated with a rhythm from the drums that had her once again swaying in her seat. Dante listened, then joined in on the piano.

"No, it needs vocals," he said after they finished. His brows drew together; then he snapped. "Let me freestyle to it."

They started again. This time, when they reached the chorus, Dante came in with vocals. Julie couldn't believe he'd freestyled right then and there.

Julie became engrossed watching them work on the music, confer together and then play again making various changes. She didn't have an artistic bone in her body but appreciated those who could make something beautiful just from the imagination. She noticed a shift in Dante the more they worked. He was less flashy, less the *I am Dante Wilson—idolize me*. He was serious about this music, jerking his clothes and rubbing the back of his neck when something wasn't working, and clapping his hands and talking excitedly when things did work.

This was the real him. The Dante who'd taken her to dinner and paid for her date with Carlos was the superstar used to getting what he wanted. This was the musician. The guy struggling to bring life to his creation. A man who cared little about his stardom when other members of the group challenged him on an idea.

This Dante impressed her, which was surprising, since she hadn't been impressed by a celebrity in years.

She wasn't sure how long they worked. It was long enough for Julie to kick off her shoes and tuck her feet under her on the couch. Watching Dante be so passionate about his music worked against her reasons not to give in to the sparks between them. His intensity, hunger and fire for what he was doing blazed in his every movement. What would having his creative talents focused on her be like? Warmth spread from her midsection, and she squirmed on the couch.

They finished a song, and Dante jumped up from the piano stool, his smile bright and eager. He'd lost the coat, and his shirtsleeves were rolled up. Every move he made was fluid—a testament to the great dancer he was. The muscles in his arms, back and shoulders flexed and tightened. Julie pictured him shirtless, moving with the same sensual grace as they made love with his shoulders bunching, arms flexing, hips pumping.

The studio door burst open. Julie snapped out of her daydream but couldn't ignore the slick evidence of exactly what she'd been dreaming about between her legs. A woman with clear brown skin, long black hair and dark eyes entered. She glanced around the room, smiled at Julie, then turned back to the guys.

Terrance put down his violin and hurried out of the studio to her. "Esha, what are you doing here?" Pleasure filled his voice.

Esha lifted on her toes and kissed him. "You're late, so I thought I'd come by and see how things were going." She turned to Julie.

Dante came to Julie's side. "Esha, this is Julie."

Esha raised a brow. "You're bringing dates to the studio now?" She looked at Julie and grinned. "You must be special."

Julie returned her smile. "That's what I keep trying to tell him."

"Well, one thing you should know is that when these

guys start working, it's hard to tear them away." She looked to Terrance. "Have you eaten yet?"

Terrance looked guilty. "I meant to eat."

Julie's stomach growled loud enough for everyone in the room to look her way. She pressed a hand to her stomach, and heat rose to her face. She'd lost her appetite after seeing all of Dante's conquests at the restaurant, and she'd honestly forgotten about food in her eagerness to watch Dante play.

Dante squeezed her shoulder. "I'll order something. There are take-out menus in the office next door. Any requests?"

The guys called out various things from pizza to Chinese. Dante looked to her. "I'll figure something out. Come with me."

He held out his hand, and she took it. They left the studio to go into the office across the hall. He went to a desk, opened the top left drawer and pulled out several menus.

"Sorry I didn't feed you," he said. "I got caught up in the music."

"I knew you were talented, but that was great."

He looked up from the menus. "Thank you. I want to go mainstream with it, but everyone thinks it'll fail."

"Everyone thought I was crazy for leaving Nexon-Jones, but here I am. Opening a nightclub with one of the world's biggest superstars."

"Point taken." He slowly flipped through the menus, then looked up again. "How did you know it would work out? Leaving your job and striking out?"

She shrugged. "I didn't know. All I knew was that if I didn't try, I'd hate myself. I could've easily gone to another firm, but I would still be at the mercy of another person. Before I chose that route, I had to see if my dream could support me."

"I worry about my career. One bad album, one wrong move, and the people hate you. Being a success is all I know."

"Being a success takes risks to be appreciated. Easy success means you take it for granted and don't know how to handle things if your success goes away."

He gave her his sexy smile, dropped the menus and came around the desk. "Is that why you're making me earn my time with you?"

"Partly. I just like to weigh options and know what I'm stepping into. I've been blindsided in relationships before. I stick to certain rules to avoid being played again."

He frowned. "What kind of rules?"

"Nothing important." She didn't want to think of all the rules that would support her walking out of this room and forgetting the route her mind had taken just a few minutes before.

He leaned close. "Am I playing by your rules?"

"At the start of the night, you were running the game plan I fully expected."

He took another step closer. His cologne seemed stronger, more intense, but she knew the heat from his body and the fire in his eyes had her acutely aware of everything about him.

"Was I?"

She nodded. "Yes, but then you brought me here. I wasn't expecting to see…you." She closed the distance between them and reached up to place a hand on his face. "I wouldn't mind getting to know you. I shouldn't—doing so breaks too many rules. I should have moved on by now."

He wrapped his arm around her waist. "Well, if you're breaking rules for me, I might as well go all in."

He kissed her long, slow and deep. Julie's hands wrapped around his neck while one of her legs snaked around his. She couldn't get close enough. She was hot, inside and out. On fire for Dante and in no mood to ignore how she felt. Strong hands gripped her and lifted as Julie's legs wrapped around his waist. He spun, never breaking the kiss, and sat her on the desk. Her hands were at the front of his shirt, pulling and tugging to get the buttons open. Dante gripped her hips, then slid his hands down her thighs. Why in the world hadn't she worn a skirt? She wanted to feel his hands on her skin.

She got the buttons free and slowly pushed the material aside. He pulled back, his nostrils flared and his lips parted with heavy breaths. The low lights in the office played with the hills and valleys of his sculpted chest and stomach and gleamed off the platinum chain around his neck. Julie ran her fingers over his chest. The muscles jumped, and she pulled her lower lip between her teeth. Feeling daring, she pinched one of his flat nipples. Dante's eyes narrowed. He groaned, grabbed the back of her head and kissed her again.

She met his fever with her own. Her tongue sliding across his, hands gripping his body, hips pressing forward. Dante cupped her breast, and Julie pushed into his palm. He toyed with the hardened tip, tendrils of pleasure flowing with each pull. Her fingers stopped their exploration of his naked chest and lowered to cup his arousal.

Dante pumped his hips forward. "You want that?" he asked, his voice deep and primal.

"I want you," she said against his lips.

The sound he made—a mixture of excitement, need and urgency—made her heart race. He found the zipper on the side of her jumpsuit and tugged the small device down. Julie pushed one sleeve off her shoulder.

The door opened. "Whoa, hey, my bad!" She heard Terrance's voice, followed by the quick snap of the door closing.

Julie and Dante froze. The interruption took all of ten seconds but was just the douse Julie needed. Dante pulled back. His eyes were bright with desire, his body tense and his arousal hard—hard and still in her hand. Julie jerked her hand away. She sucked in air and tried to think. She could not have sex with him on a desk in some unnamed studio.

Oh, a named studio would be better?

Julie closed her eyes and shook her head. "We should order food."

She opened her eyes. Dante's were closed. Slowly, he backed away, took a deep breath and then looked at her. She lost her breath, so common around him, even more so when he looked like he wanted to push her back on the desk, make her chant his name and speak in tongues.

"Okay," he said softly.

Julie nodded and slid forward on the desk. He stopped her before she got off and leaned in to kiss her gently. "Three times you've kissed me, Julie. I'll be up all night dreaming about the fourth."

Chapter 11

Dante was in the middle of his Thursday morning session with his choreographer when his cell phone rang. Annoyed by the interruption, he considered ignoring the call. The idea that the caller may be Julie sent him to the phone.

"Let me check that," he said to Armando. Wiping his face with a towel, he crossed the room to his cell. His dad's number was on the screen.

"What are you doing?" Otis asked after Dante answered the phone.

"I'm in the middle of practicing a new routine."

"Why do you sound so winded?"

Dante took a sip from the bottle of water he had sitting on the floor next to where his phone had been. "I'm not winded." He took a deep breath. "That's like admitting the moves I made ten years ago are harder now."

Otis laughed. "That's the damn problem with old age. Everything starts creaking and popping, but you don't have anything to worry about. You've got at least another ten years before your body really starts to rebel."

"That's why I keep working out now. I want to make that a lot more than ten years."

When he was a kid and his parents first insisted he learn tap, jazz and hip-hop dance, he'd hated it and thought dancing was for girls. Later he appreciated the lessons. Dancing boosted his star appeal, and he'd learned quickly how much women loved a man who could dance.

"That's what I'm talking about. We've always got to look to the future to ensure W. M. Records has staying power, which brings me to the reason for calling. Antwan will be out your way this weekend. We're close to getting him to sign, but he still wants to do a collaboration with you on his first album. I want you to get with him next weekend. Go to the studio, and see what you can come up with."

Dante gritted his teeth and squeezed the bottle in his hand. "Dad, I told you. I'm working on my own project right now. I'll be in the studio with Strings A Flame this weekend."

Otis's disgusted grunt came through the phone. "Those classical guys. Dante, you're better than that."

"They're not classical guys. Just because they play the violin doesn't mean they can't put together some really hot music."

"Look, son, hip-hop and Mozart don't go together. You've always been a strong R&B and pop star, and I think this collaboration with Antwan will strengthen your appeal to the hip-hop crowd, as well."

"I'm already strong in that market. I don't need to fully cross over. I don't mind the occasional collaboration with a rap artist, but I'm not a rapper."

"I know that. None of us are. Your sister made sure of that," Otis said bitterly. "But you know what I told you about last year's profits. We need to get ahead of where the music's trending. Right now the trend is music that Antwan is putting out. You're coming strong after the concert tour. Follow up that success with a bang by collaborating with one of the biggest names in rap instead of playing with two fiddlers on music that won't go anywhere."

He had no words to refute his dad's argument. Dante was making headway on his own project, and he wasn't ready to give up his work. "You have to at least hear the music before you toss it out."

"Your mom dragged me to enough symphonies in my life to know that I don't like it."

"But this isn't symphonic music. This is fusion—"

"I don't like fusion. Why does everyone think they need to mix stuff up all the time?"

Dante rubbed his temple with his free hand. Didn't his dad realize that mixing hip-hop and R&B was a form of fusion?

"You need to give it a try. If I were mixing jazz or the blues into my music, you'd be okay."

"Because that's music that gets people moving, music that inspires emotions and makes you want to dance. The only thing a violin can do is make you want to sleep."

"Then why did you insist I learn to play the instrument?"

"Because being successful takes more than just singing. I've always encouraged you and your sister to be multitalented. Singing, dancing and creating songs that people want to party to are your strong points. I won't have you wasting your talents on music that won't go anywhere."

Dante's head hurt, and he wanted to pound his fist into the wall. Arguing with Otis was useless. Not once had his dad tried to even hear the music Dante wanted to put together. He was always brushing it off as boring or not sellable.

He'd have to do this album on his own. W. M. Records wouldn't support it. He made a mental note to call his lawyer, who thankfully wasn't paid for by Otis and was loyal to only Dante. He'd check his contract and make sure he'd be okay to put out the music himself when the time came.

"I spoke with your sister," Otis said easily, as if he hadn't just dismissed his son's dream. "She's thinking of putting out some new music. I'm trying to get a good songwriter, and we've got the publicity department working on her rebranding. Repairing a career once it's broken takes a lot of work."

Correcting his sister's career mistake was going to take a lot of rebranding and publicity. Images of losing his status, scorn and ridicule, and becoming a laughingstock of an industry that had embraced him since he was a kid, flashed through his mind. Success meant nothing if you didn't struggle for it. Julie's philosophy sounded well and good when he was in the studio, pumped up on the music they created. What if Otis was right, and the music he was making with S.A.F. was unsuccessful and scorned?

"Tell Antwan to give me a call when he's in town," Dante said. He thought about how he could work in a few sessions with Antwan along with S.A.F. It would be difficult but doable.

"Good. I will." His dad's smug voice came through.

Dante bristled, feeling like he'd just caved. "I may even have a party on Saturday."

"Where?"

"My place. I'll also invite a few musicians—make it kind of an impromptu jam session. We'll see if Antwan and I can come up with something good for that." And he'd invite S.A.F. and test out the songs they'd put together.

"Excellent. I'd try to skip out on this trip to New York to come out and see that, but your mom is looking forward to seeing her brother."

"That's no problem. Just make it out in time for the club opening."

"When will that be?"

"A few months out, but things are coming fast. The permits are already applied for."

He talked to his dad for a few more minutes about the club. Otis didn't have a problem with Dante opening his own place. Mostly because he probably didn't believe it would be a place for Dante to showcase the classical–hip-hop fusion music he loved and would be another venue for W.M. artists. Dante couldn't deny the fear of failure. His dad's years of experience in the music industry was a cold, hard truth that he really didn't want to face, but he also couldn't give in completely. He'd throw the party and invite a few music bloggers and other celebrities. He'd kept his music to himself for too long. Time to introduce some of his fans to what he ultimately wanted to do.

Chapter 12

Unlike her previous visit to Dante's home when she'd wanted to choke him for ruining her date with Carlos, this time Julie didn't care about Carlos, or anyone else. She looked forward to seeing Dante. She hadn't seen him much during the day over the past few weeks. She'd had too many meetings with the architect and contractor, preparing the plans for submittal to the city along with her constant contact with Evette on their other projects to have enough time to see him. He had called a few times and asked her to come down to the studio and listen to him and S.A.F. in the evenings. She'd gone and left before she found herself on the desk with him again.

Valet attendants handled the parking, but Julie didn't have to worry about that because Dante had sent a car to pick her up. A pleasant surprise that she also knew was his way of making sure she came to the party.

It would also control, to some extent, when she left. He needn't worry. After seeing the less flashy side of Dante, and the more she realized he was afraid of what people would think about his music, she'd relaxed her guard.

Julie arrived well after the party was scheduled to start, not wanting to appear too eager to see him, and she wasn't surprised by the crush of people in his place. If the pool party she'd stumbled into was a last-minute thing, she expected that something planned would be elaborate. There were celebrities, hired security and waitstaff. The appetizers could have been served at a five-star restaurant instead of what was ultimately a house party.

Outside was just as dazzling. A stage was set up next to the pool, which was a brilliant blue, thanks to the lights that brightened the water. She couldn't hear the ocean over the music, sounds of laughter and constant popping of champagne bottles, but she could smell the salty air on the warm breeze.

"Hey, Julie." Esha's voice came from her left.

Julie turned and smiled at Esha, who had her arm around Terrance's waist. Julie was used to attending functions alone, but a wave of relief rushed through her from seeing someone she knew in the sea of Hollywood elite.

"Familiar faces, finally," Julie said.

Esha nodded. "I'm glad you made it. Dante was starting to worry that you wouldn't come."

Julie turned her head and toyed with her dangling gold earring to hide her delighted grin from those words. "I was just running late."

Terrance held a beer in his hand and gestured toward the stage. "Now that you're here, he'll be ready to start the show."

"Show?"

"He wants to perform the song we've been working on but didn't want to do it until you were here."

More happiness bubbled up inside Julie. This time she didn't turn away. "Where is he? I'll let him know I'm here."

Terrance pointed to the other side of the pool. "Right over there."

Julie turned in the direction Terrance indicated. Dante stood talking to another guy whose back faced her. Dante wore distressed styled jeans that probably cost enough to feed a family of four for a month, and a black V-neck shirt. He looked casual and sexy. He looked up as if sensing her gaze. Awareness jolted down her spine when their eyes met. He stopped talking and grinned at her.

If she'd known he'd greet her arrival with that smile, she would have gotten here an hour earlier.

She started in his direction. He met her halfway. "Julie, you made it." Relief filled his voice. He took her hands in his.

"Of course, why wouldn't I?"

"I don't know—you always surprise me."

"Well, I couldn't miss your debut."

Dante chuckled as his thumbs brushed the backs of her hands. "I've been performing since I was thirteen. This is hardly a debut."

"It's the debut of your new music. That's a big deal."

He nodded, glanced around and shifted from foot to foot. "Yeah. It is."

Julie tilted her head to the side. "Hey, are you okay?"

"Of course. Why wouldn't I be?" His voice held all the bravado that she expected from Dante Wilson, the superstar, but underneath there was something else.

"You're afraid."

He scoffed. "Hardly." He released her hands. Julie reached out to grip his arm, which was hard and tense.

"It's okay to admit it. You put everything into this music. Now you're letting the world see a piece of you that they've never seen before. If you weren't a little bit afraid, I'd think you were heartless," she said softly.

The tension left Dante's arm. The corner of his mouth lifted, and he met her eyes. "I'm far from heartless. If I were, I wouldn't feel so mixed up over you."

Warmth spread up Julie's face, and her breathing stuttered. He didn't mean that, couldn't mean the words. While she wanted to try to guess his angle, guess what his ulterior motive was, she couldn't. Not when he gazed at her with such sincerity, when he seemed just as baffled by the feelings stirred up when they were together.

"Well, well, well, if it isn't Julie Dominick," a male voice said.

Julie's gaze swung to the left. *Antwan?* Her stomach tightened. Her palms got slick with sweat. What the hell was he doing here? She'd seen him only twice since the opening of his nightclub—the night when the three other women he'd been sleeping with showed up. Julie's body went ice-cold. She was over Antwan and avoided guys like him. Or she had until flexing her rules and getting closer to Dante.

Don't just stand here like an idiot.

"Antwan," she said with a short head nod.

Antwan was cute, but his swagger and confidence

made him downright irresistible. He wore a pair of dark jeans and a shirt along with a red plaid button-up over the ensemble and a gaudy platinum-and-diamond chain.

"Julie," he said in a slick voice that held too many memories she'd like to forget. "I didn't know you were out here." His tattooed hand rubbed his chin. Julie thought he'd added more. God, to think she'd once pressed that hand to her heart. It made her stomach lurch.

"I'm partnering with Dante and Raymond on a new nightclub."

Dante looked between the two. "You know each other."

Julie nodded. "I helped Antwan open a nightclub in Atlanta."

"That's right. I remember Raymond said something about that."

Antwan shifted and regarded Julie with an affection that she knew was all for show. "Julie and I used to date."

"A long, long time ago," she said.

Dante pointed at Julie, then Antwan, and frowned. "You two dated?"

Well, at least she could rule out that Dante and Antwan had shared secrets about her. "Like I said, years ago." She regarded Antwan. "What brings you to Malibu?"

Antwan nodded toward Dante. "We're working on an album together."

Julie turned to Dante. "Really?"

"We're thinking about it. Antwan's considering

signing with my family's label, and it's only natural we'd consider a collaboration."

"What about your music?"

Antwan laughed. "It will be his music. He'll write the song—I'll do the rap. In fact, Dante and I are going to perform tonight. Give a little test run of what we can do together."

Julie turned back to Dante. "Terrance said you were doing another song."

Dante nodded. "We are after I indulge Antwan. Why don't you grab a drink and sit close to the stage? I want you to see both and tell me what you think."

He sounded as if her opinion was important to him, which started a fluttery feeling in her stomach. "Sure."

"Good seeing you, Julie," Antwan said. He ogled every one of her assets highlighted by her sleeveless cranberry-colored minidress, lingering on her thighs and cleavage. His gaze was both familiar and unwanted. "I really hope we can catch up while I'm in town."

Julie barely refrained from rolling her eyes; she did, however, give him an uninterested smirk. "Don't count on it."

Antwan snickered. "Why? You hooking up with Dante now, or is Raymond still sniffing around, keeping other men away?"

Anger shot up Julie's spine. Her eyes narrowed, and she prepared to tell Antwan just where to go when a tall beauty that Julie recognized as a model hurried over and threw her arms around Dante's shoulders.

"Thank you for inviting me," she said in a sexy purr and kissed his cheek.

Dante's lips curved into a tight smile that didn't

DO YOU WANT TO GET REWARDED WITH FREE BOOKS?

HARLEQUIN®
My Rewards

Join today.
It's fun, easy, and free...

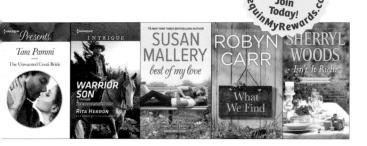

REWARD THE BOOK LOVER IN YOU WITH HARLEQUIN MY REWARDS

Here's How It Works:

Earn FREE BOOKS Join Today! HarlequinMyRewards.com

1

Sign Up!
It's free and easy to join!
Register at **www.harlequinmyrewards.com**

2

Start Earning Points!
Get 2000 points** right
now just for signing up.

3

Claim your Rewards!
Get FREE BOOKS, GIFTS and MORE!

Join today and get a FREE Book!
HarlequinMyRewards.com

**Offer ends 09/31/16

reach his eyes as he pulled the model's arms from around him. "Alicia, hey, when did you get here?"

"Just now. And guess what?" She turned and used her finger to tell another equally tall and beautiful woman to come over. "I brought my sister. Maybe we can relive Vegas." The sister came over and plastered herself on Dante's other side, putting a matching lipstick print on that cheek.

"I'm down for that," the sister said in an equally enticing voice.

Antwan howled with bawdy laughter. "Damn, Dante, you party like that?"

As the girls laughed, Dante glanced at Julie. Julie took a step back. The rose-colored glasses that she'd seen Dante through crashed to the ground. No matter what she thought she'd seen in him over the past few weeks, this was the real him—a partying playboy who would probably treat her just as casually as Antwan had.

"You guys have fun. I'm going to get a drink." She turned her back on the disgusting display and hurried to the bar.

Carlos sat on the edge of the bar. He raised his hand in a friendly wave when they made eye contact. She hadn't talked to him since their date. There were no sparks there, but for now, she was happy to have a conversation with a guy without the sparks and flutters that caused her to make dumb decisions.

Carlos pushed out the stool next to him, and she gladly accepted. "Thanks."

"I was hoping you'd be here tonight," he said.

"Why is that?"

"I enjoyed our first date." She raised a brow, and he

held up a hand. "The ending was different, but before that, it was very nice." He leaned over, placed his hand over hers and squeezed.

"I had a good time, too." She pulled her hand, but his tightened.

"Maybe we'll get together again sometime. Unless Dante won your affections."

Julie refused to look back at Dante and the wonder twins clinging to his side. "Does it look like Dante has won my affections? We work together. That's all."

Carlos let go of her hand. "Good to know. How about tonight's our do over? And we end things the way I'd hoped we would have the first time?"

"How did you want things to end?"

He waved at the bartender, pointed at his drink, then held up two fingers. "I'll just say a lot differently than they did."

The music lowered, and the crowd cheered. Julie swiveled toward the stage where Dante and Antwan were.

Antwan took the microphone. "As some of y'all know, I'm considering moving over to W. M. Records. When that happens, you'll get a lot more of what you're about to experience. Let's do this."

The DJ cranked up the music, and Dante's smooth tenor started the song. Julie had to admit, Dante's vocals and Antwan's rapping was hot. The crowd loved them together. Any song they put out would be a sure-fire hit. Would he really give up a chance for another almost guaranteed hit to make an album with S.A.F.?

They finished, and, of course, the partygoers went wild and begged for more. Dante grinned, his brow glistening with sweat from his exertion.

"Hold up, hold up," he said to the crowd. "I've got something else I want you all to hear." Terrance, Tommy and the rest of the group came up onstage. "This is something new that I'm trying. Tell me what you think."

Julie was a ball of nerves. Her heart pounded, and her stomach twisted as if she were the one debuting new music. Dante looked across the space directly at her. His eyes filled with the same nervousness that fluttered in her stomach. She lifted her glass to him in salute. Dante raised his chin, then started the music.

Instead of watching him, Julie gauged the reaction of the people at the party. There were looks of confusion when the violins started, but there was also curiosity. When the drums and bass picked up the beat, the confusion gave way to enthusiasm. Before long, the rest of the partygoers were bobbing their heads and moving to the music. When they finished the song, the crowd was on their feet, clapping and cheering.

Julie put her drink down and clapped with them, a huge smile on her face. If Dante needed a boost to tell him this was what he should be doing, then he'd gotten just that. He glanced at her, his grin so big and triumphant that her heart stuttered in her chest. She turned to get her drink off the bar to raise to him.

Her hand bumped against Carlos's. She turned, frowning, as he pulled his hand away from her glass. His smile was apologetic. "Sorry, I was trying to move the glass out of the way."

"Was it in your way?"

He shook his head. "No, the bartender was wiping things down."

She glanced at the bartender, who was wiping the

bar but was not near them. Still, he could have been right behind her when Carlos tried to move her glass.

"No harm, no foul," she said.

She took the glass, then turned back to Dante and raised it. His joy from earlier was gone. He scowled at her, then turned his glower on Carlos. He couldn't possibly be upset that she was sitting with Carlos. If anything, *he* deserved the angry stare after he'd had two supermodel sisters offer up their favors to him so blatantly. Here she was, once again, getting caught up into thinking there was more to him than she'd originally expected just because his music moved her.

She took a sip from her drink and turned back to Carlos. "How did you enjoy the music?"

Carlos looked from her glass to her. "I liked it okay, but it's nothing like the music we played on tour. I think they should just stick to that."

"Really?"

"Just my opinion. But, hey, who knows what catches on and what doesn't? I wish him well." He picked up his drink and held it out to her. "A toast to his success."

Julie touched her glass to his. "To his success," she said, taking another sip. She glanced at the stage. One of the model sisters had jumped up and was trying to plaster herself against Dante. Dante still glared at Julie. Heat spread up her cheeks. *God, I'm ridiculous. Blushing, again, just because he's looking at me.*

Julie downed her drink. Time to go before she became even more wrapped up in the crazy feelings he evoked in her.

She smiled at Carlos. "I think I'm going to call it a night."

He pouted, odd for a grown man. "That sounds like

a goodbye. I thought we were making tonight our do over."

"I'll have to take a rain check on that. I'm really not in the mood for partying." Or watching Dante scowl at her when she talked to another man while simultaneously having a supermodel trying to jump his bones on stage.

"Let me at least walk you to the door."

"There's really no need."

"I don't mind." He gave her a cute smile. "Maybe I'll convince you to let me drive you home."

"I'll let you walk me to the door, but driving me home isn't necessary." She stood.

"You said that about walking you to the door, but you changed your mind." His voice carried too much confidence that she would let him take her home. Too bad for him; she wasn't in the mood for any guy to try to sweet-talk his way into her pants.

She couldn't bear to look back at Dante and see him probably fawning over the two models. Instead she waved at Esha and headed to the door.

"You really should let me drive you home," Carlos said. "You've been drinking."

Julie's lip twisted. "Only two. Besides, Dante sent a driver, so I'm good either way."

"Are you sure?"

"Positive." Her footing slipped on the way into the house. The lights danced, and her vision went blurry. "What the…"

Carlos quickly wrapped an arm around her waist to steady her. "Are you okay? You drank a lot. I couldn't let you drive home like this."

His voice was raised. The sound made her head

throb. She pressed a hand to her temple. The people, lights and furnishings all spun like a merry-go-round. Her stomach churned. She hadn't drank enough for this to happen.

"I'm…okay."

"No, you're not. I'll make sure you get home, okay?"

He sounded way too eager. Carlos pressed her closer to him, his hand resting on the side of her breast, his thumb caressing her through her dress. The churning in Julie's stomach intensified.

"What did you put in my drink?" Her voice slurred.

He leaned close to her ear. "Just something to make you a little friendly. Don't worry—you won't remember anything tomorrow." His hot breath blew in her ear.

A tremble of fear and disgust racked her body. *No.* This could not be happening. "No!" She tried to yell, but again her voice came out sluggish and slow.

"Yes," he said in a louder voice. "You can't drive like this. I insist." He dragged her to the door, and she was too sick to stop him.

The room spun faster; then the weight of Carlos's body was gone. Julie slumped against the wall. Loud, angry male voices rang out to her left. Her head felt as heavy as a bowling ball, but she managed to drag it up. Dante was in Carlos's face. In slow motion, she watched Dante's arm pull back, then forward. His fist landed on the side of Carlos's face. Julie's eyes would have widened if they didn't feel like thick velvet curtains.

The room continued to spin, and the edges of her vision blackened. Her stomach pitched and rolled. Saliva filled her mouth. She was going to be sick. She slid down the wall. Strong arms swooped her up. No, too fast. She sucked in a breath. *Dante.* She'd recognize his scent anywhere. Her heart rate slowed. For a second, she felt safe, before throwing up the drink and everything else she'd had that night.

Chapter 13

What happened last night?

The words hit Julie's brain before a splitting head-ache took hold. She squinted her eyes even though her room was dark and slowly rose to a seated position. Her mouth felt like dirty cotton and tasted worse than that. Pushing back the plush covers, she eased her legs over the side of a bed.

Two blinks later, her vision cleared and several things became apparent at once. (A) She was not in her hotel room; (B) she was naked except for a sleeve-less T-shirt; (C) the shirt did not belong to her.

Running her fingers through her short hair, she looked around the room. There was a humongous bed covered in rich, royal blue sheets, dark masculine fur-nishings, a colossal flat-screen television along one wall hooked up to a gaming system, platinum records on another. The last wall was nothing but floor-to-ceiling windows dimmed to an opaque that she was sure turned clear with a push of a button to provide a view of the ocean. Even without the decor, she would have known she was in Dante's bedroom. The sheets smelled like him, seductive and inviting, and after spending the night in his bed, she smelled like him.

A bottle of water and ibuprofen were next to each other on the nightstand with a note that read, "You'll need this."

"What did I do?" she murmured to herself. She grabbed both and downed three pills and half the bottle of water. She paused to take a physical check of herself. She didn't feel like she'd spent the night having sex. She just felt hungover. The inside of her elbow was sore. She glanced down at the Band-Aid there. When she pulled it off there was no sign of an injury. Add that to the list of mysteries. Her stomach growled, and she was hungry.

She stood quickly. Her stomach rolled; her head spun. She took a deep breath and both cleared. *Okay, maybe too much to drink.* She glanced around the room. No sign of her clothes. If she'd come to bed with Dante after drinking too much, she would expect to see her clothes strewn over the floor in a haphazard attempt to get them off.

Where in the world is Dante?

She went into what she guessed was the bathroom and sighed with relief at the sight of the enormous gray marble shower and bathtub. The time to worry about what she'd done the night before could wait. She stripped off the shirt and got into the large shower. While she washed away the grogginess, she tried to remember how she'd ended up in his bed. Antwan had been there. Dante was thoroughly enjoying the sexy sisters eager to please him. Shouldn't they be in his bed? She dropped the soap.

For the life of her, she hoped her inhibitions hadn't dropped that much the night before!

Picking up the soap, she finished her shower. No matter how hard she pushed her brain, the only thing she remembered was sitting at the bar, saluting Dante after his performance and then having a brief conversation with Carlos. Hadn't she told him she was leaving? If so, why was she here?

Only one way to know. Find Dante.

She got out of the shower. Thankfully, there was toothbrush still in the package inside one of the multitude of drawers surrounding the sink. She wrapped a towel around herself and searched for her clothes. When she still couldn't find them, Julie said to hell with it and went into Dante's closet. The closet was the size of a mini-boutique and set up like one, too. There were cushioned stools, a wall of various loafers and sneakers and all of Dante's clothes lined up neatly on racks behind glass doors. She opted for a black T-shirt and, since his pants would be too long, a pair of starched white boxers.

"If we slept together, then I might as well get over feeling guilty for wearing his clothes."

Julie left his bedroom and stopped. Half a dozen people were upstairs cleaning up the mess from the previous night. The movement of so many people was a surprise compared with the absolute silence in Dante's bedroom. She gave them tight nods, then hurried downstairs, where another half dozen were cleaning. A woman sweeping up broken glass at the foot of the stairs glanced up at Julie and smiled.

Julie cleared her throat and tugged on the bottom of the T-shirt, which covered the boxers. Great, she had to do the walk of shame in front of the entire cleaning crew. "Is Dante around?"

The woman shook her head. "You must be Julie. Dante had to go out for an appointment, but he asked that you stick around until he gets back. He wants to make sure you're okay."

Why wouldn't she be okay? *Maybe because you woke up in his bed and don't know how you got there.* Exactly why she wouldn't leave until she found out the hows and whys of last night.

"Thank you," she said to the lady as she made her way to the kitchen.

Sunlight streamed through the large windows and gleamed brightly off the white marble countertops. Julie almost felt bad for pulling out items to make a sandwich in the middle of the cleaning efforts, but her growling stomach couldn't be ignored. She quickly put together a sandwich, then searched for someplace to hide until Dante returned, someplace other than his bedroom.

The only room where there wasn't any cleaning going on was in his home theater. Setting her food on one of the plush seats, which was more like a couch than anything, Julie searched for something to watch in the media tower next to the large screen.

"Musicals," she said with delight. As a fan of classic movie musicals, she was pleasantly surprised by his choices. She slipped in one of her favorites, *Singin' in the Rain*. After another five minutes of figuring out the blasted player and sound system, Julie settled in.

She was almost halfway through the movie, at the scene where Gene Kelley did his famous dance routine in the rain, when the door to the theater opened and Dante walked in. She took one look at him and gasped. His right eye was blackened and his jaw was bruised. Julie jumped up from her seat and rushed over.

"What happened?" She placed her hands on his cheeks and turned his head to get a better look. "Who hit you?"

He took her hands in his and lowered them, concern filling his eyes. "Forget about me—how are you? Do you need me to call a doctor?"

Julie frowned. "Doctor? For what? You're the one with the black eye."

"You don't remember what happened?"

"Did I do that to you?"

The concern in his face gave way to a small grin. "I think you did want to hit me at one point last night, but you didn't do this."

"Then who did?"

Dante's nostrils flared. His hands clenched hers almost painfully. "Carlos."

Julie twisted her hands until his grip loosened, but he didn't let her go. "Carlos? Why?"

"He didn't like it when I stopped him from taking you away from the party. I thought I saw him slip something into your drink, but I couldn't be sure from where I was on the stage. When you walked to the door and stumbled, I knew I wasn't mistaken. He was practically dragging you to the door, pretending as if you were drunk and as if he was being a Good Samaritan by driving you home."

Julie's headache and sick stomach had settled after the ibuprofen and food, but a nauseating feeling twisted her midsection. They'd been talking, and his hand had moved her glass. She'd thought that was weird...then she could barely remember going to the door.

Her eyes rose to Dante. "He drugged me?" Anger hardened her voice. "I'm going to kill him."

"He's already been taken care of." Her brows rose, and he shook his head. "No one killed him, but between me, S.A.F. and Antwan, he got the shit beat out of him before we called the police. I had to meet with my publicist this morning to handle damage control. I'd invited several reporters and music bloggers to the party to hear my new music. Carlos's stunt, and the subsequent fight, obviously overshadowed everything at the party."

"I'm so sorry."

"Don't be. What happened wasn't your fault, and I don't regret the fallout." He brushed her short bangs to the side and ran his fingers down her face. The tenderness in his eyes started a yearning deep in her chest.

"How did I end up nearly naked in your bed?"

Dante dropped his hands and grimaced. "You were falling, so I picked you up. I think too fast because you threw up."

Julie pressed her face into her hands. "Eww!"

"Tell me about it," he said with a laugh. "I took you to my room. Esha cleaned you up and put you to bed. She sat with you while the doctor checked you out. He drew your blood. The police will need to test it for the drug to have a case against Carlos."

She touched her arm where the Band-Aid had been. Mystery solved. "You called a doctor?"

"I wanted to make sure you were okay. My doctor lives nearby. If I would have shown up at the hospital with you it would have been a media circus. After I threw everybody out and dealt with the police, I came up and watched you all night."

Julie lowered her hands to stare at him. "You stayed with me all night? Why?"

"I was pretty sure whatever he gave you would just knock you out, but I didn't want you to get sick again and no one be there."

He said the words as if fighting for her honor, calling a doctor and keeping vigil at her bedside was the most natural thing. Briefly she considered a life where Dante was the man who always looked out for her, protected her and stayed beside her all night. She liked the idea.

"Thank you," she said softly.

Sex was always her choice and never entered into lightly. Before taking any guy to bed, she weighed all the consequences. After being played for a fool, she'd taken control of her dating life, her heart, her emotions and her body. In the blink of an eye, Carlos had almost stolen that from her—a blow she wasn't sure how she would have recovered from.

Trembles racked her body, tears burned her eyes and thoughts of what could have happened carved their way in vivid and bitter detail through her brain. Blinking rapidly to stop herself from crying about what might have been, Julie met Dante's eyes. "Thank you so much." Her voice cracked.

Dante cupped her face in his hands, his thumbs brushing her cheeks. Concern filled his dark eyes again, and she saw some of the same fear she felt. If he hadn't seen what Carlos had done…if he hadn't followed her to the door…

"Julie, I had no idea what he was capable of. He almost…" His hands on her face tensed, and his eyes burned with focus. "If he would have hurt you, I would have killed him. I won't let anyone hurt you."

Maybe it was the fierce intensity in his eyes, the protectiveness in his voice or the fact that he'd been her own personal superhero the night before, but Julie wanted nothing more than to have Dante's body against hers. No analyzing the consequences, no thoughts of tomorrow or what any of this meant. Just the ability to do something *she* wanted to do.

She lifted onto her toes and pressed her lips against his. He froze, but she didn't have time for hesitation and skated her tongue across his lower lip. Strong arms clasped her tight, pulling her against his body. Dante's lips parted, and he kissed her hard. *That is more like it.* Julie pulled on the front of his T-shirt, bringing him closer. Her hips twisted and pushed forward, sliding against his quickly hardening erection, leaving no doubt about what she wanted.

Dante stepped forward, and she walked backward until her back hit the lowered screen. The lights from the movie flashed across them. The sound of music, the ballet scene, intermingled with the sounds of their heavy breaths and Julie's soft moans. Dante kept one hand on the side of her face, fingers deep in her hair, while the other skimmed down her body, leaving a trail of heat behind the touch. His deft fingers found the opening in the boxers she'd borrowed. Slipping inside, he brushed slowly back and forth across the outer folds of her core.

Sparks of heat trembled through her. Slick desire pooled where his fingers caressed. Julie sucked in a breath, and her head fell back. Firm lips kissed her cheeks, down to the side of her neck, then possessively suckled on the sensitive skin. Her legs spread, and his fingers skimmed across the sensitive bud at her center, then pulled back.

"Dante." His name on her lips was an urgent plea for more.

"Julie," he answered, sounding just as needy.

Dante grabbed the bottom of her T-shirt and lifted. Julie's arms rose so he could completely remove it and toss the shirt to the floor. He quickly pushed down her boxers. When she stood before him, covered only by the flashing lights from the movie, a sinful smile curved his lips—one that promised pleasure, seduction and decadence. Julie unbuttoned his jeans, then pushed the rough material and his white boxers past his waist. Her gaze fixed on his long, hard erection.

Dante's fingers wrapped around his length. "Julie." His voice was low, deep, possessive.

He cupped the back of her head and kissed her again with all the demand and need that had coated his voice. Julie's hand lowered to push his aside and wrapped her fingers around his shaft, caressing him with firm but gentle strokes. Dante groaned and pressed her against the screen. His kiss was deeper, more erotic.

This was what she wanted. This is what she'd wanted from the second her eyes met his over the piano—him, hot and hard against her. The fact that someone had dared try to steal her choice the night before made every kiss with Dante more precious and every caress that much more exquisite. He was *her* choice. For the moment he belonged only to her, and even though he could easily snatch her heart if she wasn't careful, right now she wanted to give him everything she could.

Dante pulled away to retrieve a condom from his pants with quick, jerky movements. Before Julie could open her mouth and beg him to hurry, his body was back on hers. Gripping her thighs, he hoisted her up and pressed her back against the screen. Julie's legs wrapped around his trim waist. The hard length of his cock pulsed against her slippery center. His mouth plundered hers, branding her and wiping away any thoughts of another. Maybe indefinitely. Dante lifted her higher and lowered his head, slipping one puckered nipple into the welcoming warmth of his mouth.

"Dante," she begged, pushing her chest forward.

He suckled her deeply and moved his hips back and forth in short, steady strokes that ran the length of his cock against the swollen nub of her sex. Tension built as her hips gyrated, and her body was drenched with need. Julie gripped his head at her breast. Her breaths came faster, harder.

Oh, God, I'm going to come.

"I want you to come," Dante replied.

Had she said that aloud? The thought was fleeting because Dante lifted his head from her breast as his hips continued their grinding in pleasurable torture. Panting his name, she gripped his shoulders and moaned louder as the pressure built higher. He kissed her, then dropped a hand to position himself at her opening. Julie shifted lower, and the tip of him slid inside. With a deep, guttural groan, Dante pushed forward, filling her completely.

Chapter 14

"So, why all the musicals?"

Dante looked away from the bunch of grapes he'd been feeding Julie. They lounged on one of the couches in the theater. Julie's head rested in his lap, and his hand gently traced across her flat stomach. *The Wiz* played on the big screen. There was a spread of fruit, cheese, crackers and juice before them. After having the most mind-blowing sexual experience of his life, he'd wanted to take her upstairs and make love to her again and again. But he wasn't sure how she really felt after the ordeal of the night before. What happened earlier had been spontaneous. He wanted to take the time to make sure she was okay, then take her upstairs and get her to make those sexy noises while he was buried deep inside her.

"Inspiration," he said, plucking a green grape from the bunch and popping the firm fruit into his mouth.

"Inspiration how?"

"Most musicals have great dance sequences. I study the dance, and then I try to master the moves myself."

"Really?" She shifted away from the screen and onto her back to look him directly in his eyes. "I thought you were more of a hip-hop dancer."

"I am, but my parents wanted me to know about all forms of dance. At first I didn't get their reasoning, but now I realize that understanding all the fundamentals is what made me better."

"Is that the same with music? You play a lot of instruments."

Her hand absently caressed his forearm. Dante liked her like this—soft, open, sexy, her eyes unguarded, her smile lazy and relaxed. Even more so, he liked the way he felt with a warm and happy Julie after he'd wiped away the fear and anger that had clouded her gaze. He'd always thrilled at the chase and celebrated the victory, but this feeling was different. He'd protected his woman and wanted to keep on protecting her.

She pinched his arm. "I asked about the instruments," she said.

"*Dominance* and *excellence* are two words as reverent as prayers in my family. With a legacy like we have, and in order to maintain our level of success, there's no room for half steps. Knowing how to play the piano isn't good enough. You have to also understand drums, strings, wind and brass. I can play the violin, saxophone and trumpet."

He didn't say it as if bragging, but there was some pride in his voice.

"Sounds like your childhood was spent in music and dance lessons. Did you ever have fun?"

He smirked and ran his hand across her short, silky hair. "Honestly, not much. Not until I had my first hit and went on my first tour at thirteen. That's when the fun kicked in. I was a kid, and the world loved me, my music and my family. I still had a rigorous schedule, but my dad loosened the strings enough to let me enjoy myself."

"Loosened the strings...yikes."

He chuckled and nodded. Then his smile drifted away. Many times he had resented the constant pressure to be great at everything until the perks of being successful kicked in. Dante would admit that he was spoiled, pampered in a way that other celebrities wouldn't understand because his family had been successful for generations. He'd never regretted or resented that part of his life until last night. He'd never thought much about the people he surrounded himself with, but someone in his group had almost hurt Julie. Time to take strong inventory of who he invited into his circle.

"I guess if they hadn't pushed me so hard, I wouldn't be where I am today," he said, setting aside his thoughts. "Right now I'm ready to do something that I really want to do. Why have an appreciation for all this music and not try something different?"

"Why the collaboration with Antwan?"

He stopped stroking her hair. Dozens of questions about her previous relationship with the rapper ran through his head. He damn sure didn't want all the details, but for the life of him, he couldn't picture how they got together. Julie didn't seem like the type to fall for a player like that.

A player like me.

Dante cleared his throat and ran his fingers through her hair again. "My dad is pushing that. W. M. Records needs a boost. We've had declining sales the past two years. Not enough to do major damage but enough for people to smell blood in the water. If I work with Antwan and get him to sign with us, it'll go a long way to keeping the stars we've got and signing new ones."

"But it'll also make working with S.A.F. harder."

He nodded. "Yeah. Choosing between my dream and my family's legacy is next to impossible. I want to do both—sign S.A.F. to our label and bring something new to the company. My dad's against it."

She was silent for several seconds. "Doing something different from what you've always done can be difficult. You almost feel as if you're going against yourself."

"You understand the feeling?"

She nodded and resettled in his lap. "I do. When I was younger I was so spontaneous. I didn't always think through all the consequences of my actions. Just listened to my gut instinct and went with that."

"Most kids are like that."

"True, but for some people, going with your first instinct can lead to trouble. For me, things always seemed to work out. That was my compass, to trust myself and to know that I could be secure in my decisions. Now I analyze everything. I wonder about the repercussions and weigh the pros and cons."

"That can be smart, especially when starting a new business."

"It's not just business—it's every aspect of my life." She frowned, frustration filling her voice. "I scrutinize everything in my personal life, every step that I take, just so I don't end up blindsided."

She turned her head to stare at the screen. Dante doubted she paid attention to the movie.

"Were you that way with Antwan?"

She blinked, looked at him, scoffed and sat up. "Why would you say that?"

He wanted to pull her back against him. "He broke your heart."

She shrugged, but the stiffness in her back proved the move wasn't indifferent. "We just weren't on the same page in our…relationship. If you'd call it that. I thought we were exclusive, and I was wrong. Guess I shouldn't have been so quick to believe a guy as famous and popular as him really meant it when he said that I was his heart, and that I was the only one for him. Even worse, I assumed that him saying, 'I want you to have my baby,' meant he wanted to marry me."

She jerked a grape off the vine and tossed the fruit in her mouth.

"Julie."

She held up a hand. "Don't. I've heard it all. 'He shouldn't have said that if he didn't mean it' or 'You're not dumb for thinking you were special to him.' Because regardless of any of the excuses, I should have paid attention to the signs. I brushed off the flirting women, numbers in his pocket and rumors of him sleeping around as part of the hassle that came with dating a celebrity. When we were together, he gave me all of his attention, but when we weren't together, he didn't reach out to me, didn't even act as if he missed me. After I realized I was one of many, and was devastated, Raymond was my only friend to be straight with me. He let me know exactly how I'd been played and how to notice the signs in other relationships. Now I strive to be clear about the expectations before going into any relationship."

Dante clenched his teeth to keep from swearing. His toe tapped against the floor while he weighed his words. He couldn't make any excuse for Antwan—hell, he *was* Antwan. He'd said and done the same things over his life as a celebrity, with the exception of the baby comment. He had whispered promises of more in the middle of sex—promises that later bit him in the ass but were quickly forgiven and forgotten.

No wonder Julie had originally pushed him away. She'd seen in him the same type of guy who'd broken her heart, no matter what she said. After last night, all Dante wanted to do was protect her heart, cherish her, but what could he possibly do to make her believe that?

"What are your expectations for us?" he finally asked.

She turned to watch him, and as he stared into her amber eyes, his heart played wildly in his chest. The smallest beat of hope that she'd felt the same connection he had when they'd made love earlier accompanied the rhythm.

"We're mixing business and pleasure…against our better judgment."

The beat died. "What if my better judgment says mixing business and pleasure with you is the right thing to do? That not being with you goes against everything in me? That something tells me this is worth exploring?"

Her lips parted. The tip of her tongue darted out across her full bottom lip. Her eyes softened for a second before her lips lifted in a teasing grin, and she shook her head.

"It's just the afterglow from earlier. We're both hyped up from last night." She popped some grapes in her mouth, then looked at him. "Don't worry—I know this isn't going to last long. Right?"

Wrong. So very wrong. He wanted this to last. But could it really? He was in California; she was in Georgia. He toured, lived his life on the road and got more numbers, naked groupies snuck into hotel rooms and invitations than Antwan could imagine. Before meeting Julie, he wasn't ready to settle down. He'd had a threesome just a few weeks ago. Now, after one time with her, he couldn't imagine spending his nights without Julie by his side.

Would she believe him? Did *he* believe himself? This type of stuff, the feeling of completeness, didn't happen after one round of sex. Could it?

He wasn't sure if he could answer the question. Not right now. For once he needed some time to think over what he expected from a relationship.

"You're right, just a little fun. Do you want to see me do the dance from one of the movies?" he asked, needing to change the subject before he blurted out his thoughts—thoughts she'd probably scorn.

What looked like disappointment flashed briefly in her eyes before she grinned. "Any one I call out, you can do?"

"I promise."

She bit her lower lip and pulled her brows together, thinking. "Hmm. I'll go with the famous sequence from *Singin' in the Rain*."

"Really? Why that?"

"Because I'm in love with Gene Kelly and his thighs. If you pull it off—" she leaned close and ran her hand up his leg, squeezing his thigh "—I might let you get in between my thighs again."

His cock went from soft and sated to half rigid and ready. Thoughts of the future could wait until tomorrow. Today he wanted Julie back in his arms. Taking her hand in his, he lifted her from the seat. "Deal."

Chapter 15

Three days later, the only thing Dante could think of was Julie. She hadn't spent the night and had chosen to go back to her hotel room after the doctor checked her out to verify she was okay and they'd made love twice more. He'd asked her to stay. When she'd insisted on leaving, he'd almost begged.

Thank God I have some pride.

Dante Wilson did not beg. He should be glad that she hadn't called in the past three days or hadn't gotten needy after they slept together. Instead he was irritated and had picked up his phone to call her too many times, only to put the thing down. He needed some distance. He would not be the dope that fell in love with a woman who guarded her heart like a navy SEAL, analyzed every move he made like a computer software program and dissected his every word as if they were a middle school science project.

"Hey, Dante, you made the blogs," Terrance said from where he sat on one of the sofas in the studio. They were the only two there. The rest of S.A.F. was not expected to show up until later that afternoon.

Dante looked up from the sheet of music he was supposed to be reading instead of wondering about his *feelings*.

"What are you talking about?"

Terrance stood and crossed the room. He gave his cell phone to Dante. "I checked out the blogs from the people at your party the other night. Instead of talking about our music, they're talking about the fight. How you and Antwan beat up the guy who drugged Julie."

"What?" He scanned the words on the screen. A few lines in, and he cursed. The blogger, Gary Mo, had gotten the gist of what happened and filled in the rest for entertainment value.

He read aloud. "Promising real estate developer Julie Dominick hit it big after opening a nightclub for her former lover Antwan and is now cozying up to Dante Wilson while helping him open a nightclub in partnership with her longtime friend and suspected lover Raymond. Sources say the fight actually started earlier in the night when Dante and Antwan were both vying for her attention. The stunt pulled by a drummer in Dante's circle sparked the animosity brewing between the two. Hopefully, Dante and Antwan won't let—" Dante gritted his teeth and took a deep breath "—*a piece of tail* ruin a collaboration that the music world is pining for."

He gripped the phone, and his arm flexed with the need to throw the damn thing. If this had been a blogger with a small following, Dante wouldn't care. But

Gary not only had a popular site about what was new in music, he also had a side job as the music correspondent for a weekend news show on a popular entertainment channel.

Dante glared up at Terrance. "This is ridiculous. He's calling what happened to Julie a *stunt*? This completely ignores the statement my publicist put out and creates a problem that isn't there."

"I know," Terrance said with a disgusted look.

"Are all of the bloggers we invited posting this?"

Terrance shook his head. "Not like this. A few talk about the music and the people there, but they do, eventually, go into the fight. That's the highlight of every story. This is the first one I read that went into Julie's history with Antwan."

"Anyone reading this will think I'm working with her because I'm sleeping with her and not because she was the best person for the job."

Dante's shoulders bunched, and he slapped the phone back into Terrance's waiting hands, guessing his friend knew he was close to smashing it. Julie's voice was filled with pride and determination whenever she talked about why she started her own firm. The reasons for her success were the exact opposite of what Gary implied.

Dante jumped up and dug into his pocket for his cell. "I'm going to call him and tell him he's out of line."

Terrance held out his hands. "Hold up—I wouldn't do that." When Dante glared, Terrance shrugged. "Calling him will only stir the flames. You know Gary. He likes to be the first person on anything new. If you call him, he's going to take what he said to be the truth, and before you know it, the story is not just on his site but being broadcast on *Hollywood News*. The best thing to do is let this story die down. Julie is okay. Carlos got his ass kicked, was arrested and, between you and Antwan blackballing him, will never work with anyone good again. Besides, some of the bloggers had good things to say about our music."

"I don't feel right leaving things like this. Julie is the victim here, and instead of pointing that out, he's painting her as someone who has to sleep her way to the top."

"Dante, half of what's reported on a celebrity's life is a lie. You and I both know that. Julie is a big girl, and she's been around this business long enough to know how things work. She probably doesn't want any more attention brought up about this anyway. Just leave it alone."

Terrance slipped his phone into his back pocket. "I'm going to grab some lunch. Think about that while I'm gone."

Dante nodded and watched Terrance leave. He knew what Terrance said made sense. There'd been so many rumors and mistruths reported about him in the news that he spent most of his time laughing at the stories journalists came up with. This shouldn't be any different. If anything, the potential tension between him and Antwan would probably lead to more buzz about a collaboration between them.

Dante pulled out his phone and checked the sites of the other people he'd invited to the party. As Terrance said, almost all of them had good things to say about the music, but the biggest chunk of coverage was given to his song with Antwan. He wasn't surprised, but he was still disappointed. Anything he and Antwan did together would be hot. People would buy the music and flock to a concert. His career would continue to rise. W. M. Records would get the boost it needed, and other artists would sign. Though there were no negative comments about him and S.A.F., there also weren't any gushing words telling people to anticipate a new and different sound.

Intermingled with everything he read was some version of the same assumptions about him, Julie, Antwan and even Raymond. None as blatant as the one Gary wrote, thankfully. If he called Gary to get the story straight, the guy would gleefully report that Dante called him to try to shut the story down and stifle his freedom of the press, bringing more attention to his relationship with Julie. Even though she had his thoughts scattered like notes in the wind, currently the extent of their relationship was exactly what Gary reported. They'd slept together, nothing more. The thought nagged him, going against the need to protect Julie from further harm.

The best thing to do is let this story die down.

Terrance's words made his instincts rebel, but his brain held firm. He had to go with Terrance's advice to ensure this entire situation blew over. For the first time in his life, Dante didn't like what came with being a celebrity.

Julie pretended to check emails on her phone while the building inspector went through the latest renovations for Dante's nightclub. Sheila accompanied the inspector on the walk-through. From what Julie could overhear, she answered all of the inspector's questions with no problems. Still, Julie's stomach fluttered. Sheila hadn't given Julie much doubt in hiring her as the contractor for this job, and she had confidence things would go well. She needed this inspection on the electrical system to pass so they could move forward.

When the inspector and Sheila came to the front of the building, Julie slid the phone into the pocket of her suit and looked expectantly from one to the other.

"So, how did things go?" Julie asked.

Sheila didn't look at Julie. Dread landed in Julie's stomach with a heavy thud. She turned to the inspector and raised her brows.

The inspector pursed his lips before checking his notes. "You haven't sprinkled the building. You can't cover up the ceiling until that's in."

Julie's eyes widened, and she turned to Sheila. "There's no way we would have not sprinkled the building."

The inspector shook his head. "I checked, and there are no sprinklers."

"That wasn't on the plans," her contractor said.

Julie frowned. "On the plans or not, I think we should have known to install sprinklers."

"If it's not on the plans, I don't put it in. Take that up with the architect," Sheila said.

Julie ground her teeth to keep from swearing. "Did you know we would need sprinklers?"

Sheila lifted a shoulder. "I thought we might, but since it wasn't on the plans…"

Julie pressed her lips together and raised a hand. "You decided not to say anything." She would take this up with the architect, but she couldn't believe Sheila would let them get this far without saying something.

The inspector grunted. Julie turned narrowed eyes on him. "Is there anything else?"

"That's the main thing. Everything else is minor. Normally, I'd be surprised that you didn't notice they weren't installing sprinklers, but I guess I can understand why you might overlook that."

Julie's head cocked to the side and she crossed her arms. "Really, why?"

"Well." The guy chuckled. "You know," he said as he looked back at his notes.

"No. I don't know," Julie said. "Maybe you can explain why your plan reviewer didn't notice that before approving the plans." Julie didn't like to play the blame game, but if he was going to fill his voice with judgment about her capabilities, she would do the same.

The smirk disappeared from the inspector's face. "All I'm saying is the building needs sprinklers installed. If you're thinking about calling downtown to complain and get my boss to override this, save your breath. I'm calling to let him know, and I'm not signing off until I see sprinklers installed."

Julie's shoulders straightened. "I'm not calling downtown to complain. I follow the building codes on all my projects."

The guy grunted as if he didn't believe her. He tore off a carbon copy of his inspection and held it out to Julie. "Call me when the sprinklers are in." He looked to the contractor. "And don't think about closing up that ceiling beforehand. I'll get you to tear it out to prove you installed the system."

Sheila bucked up. "Do you know who's behind this project?"

"A celebrity is behind every project in this town,"

the inspector said. "That doesn't mean I'm cutting corners." He glanced at Julie. "No matter how *close* you are to Dante Wilson."

Julie glared. "My professional relationship with Dante has nothing to do with how well I do this job. We'll get the sprinklers installed."

The inspector's doubtful gaze flicked over Julie. He grunted, then turned and stomped out the door. His look annoyed her more than the issue with the sprinklers. She'd spent one day in Dante's arms, one day that no one should know about. Well, there was the cleaning crew. How many of the stories about celebrities originated with their staff? For all she knew, everyone knew that she'd spent the day having sex with Dante, annoying building inspectors included.

Julie swung back to Sheila. "Seriously? You didn't think to bring up that we needed to install sprinklers?"

"It's a renovation. I didn't think the code called for it. Besides, do you know how much money that'll cost?"

"I don't care. Do you know how many people will die if a fire breaks out and we don't have sprinklers? What type of scandal that will put on Dante's name?"

Sheila raised her hands. "Fine. I'm on it."

Julie gritted her teeth to keep from strangling the woman. She ignored the headache that started after the inspector left and focused on figuring out her next step. She wanted to put the entire blame on Sheila and the architect, but honestly, she hadn't paid nearly enough attention to the project, thanks to her preoccupation with Dante. First, the trips to his studio, followed by sleeping with him over the weekend.

She didn't regret sleeping with Dante, not really. After what almost happened with Carlos, she'd needed to, but something inside her heart had shifted when they'd made love. The mixture of hero worship for him beating the crap out of Carlos and lust from a fantastic day of sex put her very close to losing her heart. She needed space. Time to stop being distracted by Dante's dream and focus on hers before she got more looks like the inspector had given her.

Julie spent the rest of the afternoon going over the last few inspection reports and was surprised to find that this wasn't the first mention of the sprinklers. She also noted other instances where the inspector pointed out other small ways that Sheila had tried to get over on certain code requirements. By the time Julie left for the day, she'd fired Sheila and called Orlando to see if he could complete the job. He'd taken another project but would be able to send one of his crews to work for her in a few weeks.

Even though she needed to keep as much distance between her and Dante as possible, she went to his studio at the end of the day. She hated to report that she'd let something so major go unnoticed, but she didn't back away from admitting when she messed up. He needed to know Sheila was out and Orlando was taking over.

She entered the studio to find Dante and S.A.F. working on new music. The melodic sound of his voice combined with their music soothed her ragged emotions. They finished the song, and Dante immediately turned to her. The smile on his face seemed forced compared with the easy grin he'd worn while they practiced. He lifted his chin in a quick acknowledgment of her presence and looked away.

A dull pain spread through her gut. *You're right,*

just a little fun—his words, and his agreement to what she had said. She couldn't feel hurt because he didn't seem happy to see her. He'd sampled the girl; the novelty had worn off.

"Let's take a few minutes, guys," he said and came over to her. "Hey, what are you doing here?"

The question hurt. He'd never asked before—further proof he hadn't been moved by what happened between them. "Is there somewhere we can talk?"

"Sure, let's go next door." He pulled her out of the room and led her into the office across the hall. Her gaze drifted to the desk. Her mind visualized what they would have looked like the last time they were in that room together, when he'd sat her on top, kissed her and made her body yearn for more.

Tearing her eyes from the desk, she looked to Dante. He didn't meet her gaze. He sat on the edge of the desk, his brows drawn together and a pensive look on his face. It was the look of a guy who didn't want to have the weird, where-do-we-go-from-here conversation after sex. He probably thought she'd brought him in here to have a heart-to-heart about what had happened the other day.

Julie straightened her shoulders and tried to give him an I'm-cool smile. *Never act weird the day after sex. Keep things the way they were before.* Rules she'd strictly followed to prevent a guy from thinking she was getting attached.

"Look, don't get weird about what happened the other day," she said. "We both know that was just us blowing off some steam from the attraction that brewed from the moment we met. It's no big deal. We got what we wanted, and now we can work together like professionals."

Dante's pensive expression changed. His brows drew together and his eyes narrowed. Crossing his arms, he leaned forward. "I wasn't going to get weird about what happened. Why would you think I am?"

"You're avoiding eye contact, asking why I'm here. I just want to talk to you about the nightclub. Not, you know, rehash what happened. I've already moved on."

His mouth had opened before Julie finished speaking, but it snapped shut with her last remark. He took a deep breath. "You've moved on?"

"Of course. Haven't you?"

Dante scratched his chin, then ran a hand over his head. "Yeah. It's not like something magical happened."

She couldn't tell by his tone if he was mocking her or was upset. Regardless, it caused a knot in her chest. "Right. I just want you to know that I'm not expecting more."

He nodded as a line formed between his brows. "Neither was I."

They stared at each other. The silence grew to an awkward pause. Frustration and anger clenched her midsection. Did he have to sound so blasé about the entire thing?

"What did you want to talk about?" The frown on his face cleared, and he uncrossed his arms to rest his hands on the desk.

"I fired Sheila and hired Orlando today. She cut corners and was trying to get by without meeting all the codes. We almost got in trouble today with the building inspector, but I made it clear that things will be back on track. I'd hoped by the end of the week, but Orlando can't take over the job immediately."

"You did all that without talking to me first?"

"Did you want to keep a crappy contractor on the job?"

"What happened?"

"They haven't installed sprinklers. Sheila says it's because the architect didn't put them on the plans. I don't know how they were approved without that, but it really doesn't matter. We need them and can't move forward until they're installed."

"How much will this delay the opening?"

"Orlando won't be able to start for another three weeks. I know I made a big decision without talking to you or Ray, but I didn't trust Sheila to finish the job without additional issues."

He nodded, then shrugged. "It sounds like you've got things handled."

"Are you upset?"

He shook his head. "I have no doubt about your abilities. If you think firing Sheila is for the best then I'll trust you." He frowned and rubbed his temples. "Three-week delay. I guess I can live with that."

"I'll see if Orlando knows someone who can at least get the sprinklers installed before he takes over."

Dante nodded. "Do that. Maybe it'll keep us on time. Is that all you wanted to talk about?"

He sounded like he expected her to say something else. There was plenty more she wanted to say. Why did he so readily agree that the other day meant nothing? Had he really not felt something magical between them? *God, don't be silly, Julie.* The guy slept with supermodel twins regularly. Of course, an afternoon of sex with her wouldn't be life changing.

"That's it. Was there something you wanted to talk to me about?" She hoped he didn't notice the expectancy in her voice.

"Actually, there is. I thought you would have read the blog post by now."

"What blog post?"

He pulled out his phone, and, after a few swipes of the screen, he handed it to her. "This one."

Julie scanned the blog. Her muscles tightened with each word. No wonder the inspector doubted her competency. He didn't expect her to know a thing about getting the club opened correctly as long as she got publicity and the chance to warm Dante Wilson's bed.

Her head snapped up. "Are you going to correct them?"

"I've already released my statement about what happened. This is a really bad twisting of events for entertainment value. Regardless of what I say, reporters and bloggers will choose their own angle. I'm not going to say anything else."

"What? Why not?"

"Because fighting with Gary about his article will cause more harm than good. Coming to your defense will make it look like something's going on between us and support their accusations."

Something was going between them, but she refused to say that. "So you're going to let them think that I'm only here because I'm sleeping with you."

"We both know that's not true. Once you get the club opened, everyone will see that you did a great job and that it had nothing to do with our…situation."

Situation? "Fine. Do what you want." She spun on her heel and marched to the door.

Her hand touched the knob, and Dante's hand slammed into the door, preventing her from opening it. "Julie."

She took a deep breath, but instead of calming her frayed nerves, she breathed in Dante's masculine cologne. Her mind swam with memories of being wrapped up in nothing but his arms, his scent. Awareness buzzed in her midsection. "What?"

"It's killing me to not say anything."

"I'm sure it is, Dante."

He pressed closer, the heat of his body burning into her skin. "Julie, I'm furious about the way he glossed over what happened to you. Staying quiet will let this blow over faster."

She turned and faced him. He stood so close to her that her head fell back to meet his eye. "So you can get back to focusing on your music."

"No, so we don't have the media combing through your past and trying to find further justification to malign your character. I won't have them dragging your name through the mud and victim blaming you when Carlos is the one who should be ripped to shreds. Letting these rumors fade into the sunset is the best way to keep your name out of the media's spotlight. He's going to jail for what he did. And I've already taken steps to make sure Carlos never works in this business again when he's released. This is my fault. All of it, starting with trusting Carlos."

His voice vibrated with frustration and anger. Her shoulders slowly relaxed. Dante was right; another statement from him would look like he was trying too hard to justify partnering with her and would only backfire. Thanks to his decision to call the police and his doctor, if convicted, Carlos could go to jail for at least ten years. By the time the club opened, this would be a distant story in Hollywood's fleeting memory. When the club was successful, regardless of the rumors, it would go a long way to show she could handle opening larger projects.

"I don't like it, but I get it. This isn't your fault. Not really."

"I still feel terrible. I don't want to give anyone else reason to make light of what happened." He brought his hand up to the side of her face. "You're too special for that."

Her lips parted, and a soft sigh escaped her. Her heart turned mushy for him all over again. Julie shifted so that his hand fell away.

"So, I guess I can't touch you now?" His smile was easy, but his voice was tight.

Julie wished the door was open so she could step back or that Dante would move away and she could escape the seductive cocoon of his presence.

"Dante, my reputation as a developer is the most important thing to me. After I left Nexon-Jones, rumors started that I had to sleep with clients to get where I am, add to that the disaster of my relationship with Antwan after opening his nightclub, and automatically people doubt my ability to grow so fast so quickly on my own merits. This job was supposed to help Dominant Development, not hurt it."

"Don't use your business and the assumptions of other people as a reason to ignore what we both feel."

"Not hard to ignore something that isn't magical, right?" she threw back.

"What the hell am I supposed to say, Julie? You come in here claiming to have moved on. You haven't reached out to me since walking out of my place, then tell me not to get weird. Am I really supposed to admit that not only did the other day mean something to me, but that I want a whole lot more of you?"

Julie's mouth opened and closed, one hand pressed into her stomach, the other pushed against the door behind her. Words wouldn't come.

"Don't say we can't or we shouldn't be together because of the chance of rumors. Everything that I do causes rumors. That's a weak excuse."

Her eyes snapped to his. "No, it is not."

"Yes, it is, especially when you're using it as a barrier to ignore what's happening between us. I never took you for a coward, Julie."

Her chin lifted. "I'm not a coward."

"Then don't run from me now."

Dante lowered his head. His warm lips brushed hers before pushing forward, demanding more. Her lips parted, and her hands cupped his face, drawing him closer. Dante's hard body molded to hers. The kiss, deep, challenging, stealing her breath and her thoughts, tore through her instincts to do exactly what he accused her of trying to do—run far and fast before she was trapped and wouldn't be able to protect her heart.

Dante lifted her leg, settling his hips better between her thighs, and thrust his growing erection into her. Moaning low and deep, Julie's hips rolled forward.

A strong hand pulled her blouse from her pants, then slid up her side to cup her breast. His thumb rubbed her turgid nipple. "Don't run from this, Julie." His voice was a dark, husky whisper.

Julie popped open the button of his pants and jerked down the zipper. "Who's running?"

Dante's sexy grin sent thrills through her body. He kissed her again, and Julie gave in to the pleasure. Tomorrow she'd figure out her next move. Tonight she was no one's coward.

Chapter 16

Then she ran.

For the next few weeks, Julie made herself unavailable to Dante, except on her terms. She may not be a coward, but she also wasn't stupid. Her body wanted Dante, but her heart wanted in on the deal. She had to use her mind and be strategic about things. This meant focusing on getting the club opened during the day, not going to the studio every night, not coming over when he called and only having sex with him on her schedule once per week.

The only reason she'd come to his house in the middle of a weekday today was because he'd said he needed to discuss the opening. With her renewed efforts to personally double-check the work of the sprinkler installer Orlando had recommended, they were almost back on schedule, and she needed to give Dante an update. Though she didn't push away the thought that the invite could just be his way of trying to get her in his company. Dante hadn't shown signs of noticing how she was subtly handling their hookups, and if he did notice, he didn't seem to care.

Her hand hovered over the bell, but the sound of a car pulling up in the long drive behind her caught her attention. Turning, she watched Raymond park his black Ferrari next to her rental. He got out, and her smile widened.

"When did you get back?"

Raymond hurried over; his black pants and white T-shirt looked wrinkled while his gold chain flashed in the California sun. When he reached her, he pulled her into a hug. "I just got off the plane. Dante had told me you were coming over here when I couldn't reach you on the phone." After releasing her, he pulled back and scanned her from head to toe. "Are you okay?"

"Yeah, I'm fine. You're right on time. Dante wants to talk to me about the upcoming opening, and I need to give him an update on the progress of the club." She turned and rang the bell.

"Apparently so," Raymond said in a weird tone of voice.

The door opened before Julie could ask what was up with that. The same housekeeper who'd greeted her when she'd woken up in Dante's bed and wandered downstairs answered.

"Come on in," she said. "Dante received a call after buzzing you through the gate. He asked that you wait by the pool. I'll bring out some refreshments."

Julie smiled. "Thank you."

Instead of sitting by the pool, they moved to one of

the seating areas in the garden that overlooked the sparkling blue waters of the Pacific. Raymond sat next to Julie on the couch they shared, his arm resting behind her. He watched her intently, searching for something.

Julie shifted in the chair to face him. "What's wrong, Ray?"

He ran his hand over his precisely faded haircut. "Did someone really drug you?"

Julie winced; thinking that Raymond wouldn't have heard the story in another country was crazy. He followed the entertainment sites and blogs more than anyone. Even though Dante ignoring the accusations had prevented the story from blowing up, the entertainment shows had reported on the fight after.

"Yes, but nothing happened. Dante saw what he did and stopped things from getting out of hand."

Raymond rubbed his eyes. "A fight is getting out of hand." He dropped his hand. "Damn, Julie, I should have been here."

"Why? What would have changed if you were in town?"

"I would have been with you. Everyone there would have known you are my girl, and no one would have dared mess with you."

Julie held up a hand. "Whoa, wait a minute. What do you mean, your girl?"

"Come on, Julie—we both know you're my girl."

"I'm your friend, Raymond. You're one of my best friends, but that's all."

Raymond's face turned serious. "You know there's more to us than that." He dropped a hand to clasp one of hers. His palms were sweaty. "We're meant to be together."

Julie's heart jumped into her throat. "Where's this coming from, Ray?"

"I haven't forgotten the promise we made. That when we were ready, when the time was right, if we were still single, we'd be together."

"Ray, that was a promise made when I was crying and heartbroken. I never meant to hold you to it."

"Maybe you didn't, but I took it seriously." He brought her hand to his chest. "You know how I felt about you then. I still feel the same now. Julie, you're the one."

Julie stood up in a rush. She turned to the ocean and shook her head. "I'm not *the one*. Not for you."

Raymond came up behind her. "Yes, you are, and I'm the one for you. I can protect you and make sure no one ever hurts you."

Julie turned to Raymond. "Ray, you're a great friend, and I appreciate the fact that you're always there for me and that you always look out for me. I'm here with the job of a lifetime because of you. I treasure your friendship, but that's all I want. Nothing more."

"We'd be good together." He reached to rub her cheek.

Julie leaned away. "No, we wouldn't."

"How do you know that?"

"Because you taught me too well about the way men think. You're upset about what happened to me, that you weren't here for your homegirl, and thinking that means we should be together. When we both know that anything romantic between us wouldn't work. It didn't work then and wouldn't work now. You're really not ready to settle down, and I don't want to settle with you."

Raymond's face turned hard. "But you're ready to settle down with Dante?"

"No, where's that coming from?"

"There's nothing going on with you?"

She wouldn't lie to her friend. "We hooked up a few times, but there's nothing else. I know that this is just sex and not romance."

"Julie, what did I tell you? When you tell a guy that you're not looking for a relationship and are only interested in sex, then that's what the guy hears. He's not going to change his mind or suddenly fall for you."

The truthful words were a dagger in her heart. A dagger she hid behind a smile blanketed in confidence she didn't feel. "I know that."

"You deserve better than that. If I'm not ready, then I know he's not. He's not the guy who turns away the groupies on the road. If anything, he indulges in them. He's lived a life where fame, money and women all come easily."

"I know."

"Do you? Because you deserve so much more than that, Julie," Raymond said earnestly. He brushed her cheek with his hand. "You're better than just another number he can add to the long list of conquests."

Julie squared her shoulders. "Don't worry, Raymond. I'm handling the situation. You think I don't know this thing going on between me and Dante is nothing? I've been very deliberate about keeping my emotions out of things. He's a hookup, nothing more."

Her voice came out sure and confident, when inside she knew she was a liar. If she didn't have to work so hard to control this situation, then she could say every word and mean them. Seeing his love of music, his drive to try something new, even his fear of the un-known, had slowly started the process of etching his name in her heart. She feared she'd have a hard time erasing it.

"Good," Raymond said. "I don't want to see you hurt again. I love you, Julie."

Julie smiled and kissed Ray's cheek. "I love you, too, Ray." The sound of a throat clearing interrupted them.

Julie swiveled toward the sound. Dante smiled, but the look he threw her and Raymond was ice-cold.

Chapter 17

"Sorry for keeping you waiting—my dad was on the phone." Dante had no idea how he kept his voice so cool when boiling-hot jealousy coursed through him.

Julie's wide eyes glanced from him to Raymond and back to Dante. He'd heard most of their conversation, including her refusal of Raymond, and he knew her declaration of love for Raymond wasn't in a romantic sense. That didn't stop the jealousy he felt after seeing her kiss Raymond's cheek and hearing her flippantly call Dante nothing more than a hookup.

"Is everything okay?" Julie asked. Her voice was calm despite the uncertainty in her eyes.

"Yeah, things are all good." Dante strolled around the couch over to her and Raymond. "Raymond, I'm glad you're back in town."

Raymond lifted his chin. "Oh, really?"

"Yes. I was telling my dad about the plans for the nightclub, and he wants to come check out the progress. He's coming with my mom and sister next week. I'm thinking of making it a small dinner party, and I want you to come so that they can hear your thoughts. Maybe if they hear that you're interested in offering different types of music, they won't think I'm so crazy."

Raymond chuckled. "You're not crazy. I think people will flock there despite the music. You're Dante Wilson—you can have whatever you want, whenever you want."

Dante would have normally been okay with that description, but after hearing the way Raymond described him to Julie, he wondered if Raymond was using the words as another veiled warning for Julie to stay away from Dante.

"That doesn't mean I'm capricious about what or who I go for." He looked directly at Julie.

She lifted her chin as the uncertainty in her eyes turned to a mocking disbelief. He could imagine the doubts going through her mind. He didn't have much room to stand on if she were to call bull. He knew she'd pulled back in their relationship. Her actions had him standing on a sea of uncertainty. He wanted to demand that she tell him where they stood, insist that she admit her feelings and do exactly what he hated when women tried to do the same to me. He didn't need to, though, because apparently her feelings were locked safely behind those walls she put up.

Raymond shifted from foot to foot, drawing Dante's attention. "What day next week are you doing this?"

Dante forced his attention back to his parents coming to town. "They'll be here at the end of the week. I'm thinking dinner on Friday night."

"I'll be here."

Dante looked to Julie. "And you?"

"You want me to come?"

"Of course. You're our partner in this project and know more about what's happening with the renovation than I do. Knowing my dad, he'll have questions on that."

She nodded. "Sure, if you want me to be here, then I'll be here."

He wanted her there, not because she worked with him, but because, out of everyone, he knew she was the one who truly believed in his venture. Tightness filled his chest; Dante rubbed the spot. He was actually hurt by her easily tossing him aside.

Raymond's phone rang. "I need to take this." Raymond answered the phone and strolled away.

Dante crossed to Julie. "So I mean nothing to you?"

Julie turned toward the ocean. "We both knew what we were getting into."

"You're running again."

She spun to him and crossed her arms. The wind played with the ends of her bangs, and despite her angry posture, he thought she was beautiful in the tight cream-colored dress. "I'm not running—I'm being honest. Don't play games with me."

"Why do you insist this has to be a game? That I don't want more from you?"

"Then tell me what you envision for our future, Dante. Me moving to California? You moving to Georgia? You deciding that you're ready for a serious long-distance relationship? The agreement that we don't sleep with other people, and then me believing that you'll walk away when another set of eager women are waiting in your hotel room after a concert?"

"I'm not that bad, Julie."

"Aren't you? We won't work. Let's just call this what it was and move on. Don't get caught up in the moment. It's only fleeting."

"I want you to be my girl."

"That's the thing, Dante. I'm a woman, not a girl. I may open nightclubs, but I don't spend my weekends in them. I want a house and kids. I want to sit on the couch watching television and have date nights at the movies. I want a guy who works from nine to five who comes home and kisses me on the cheek, then tells me about his day at the office. Not a guy who calls from his tour bus while his entourage is partying in the background. Tell me you want that, and then we can talk."

He didn't. Not the version she spouted off. "I don't." Her jaw clenched, and pain flashed in her bright amber eyes before she looked away. "But you don't either."

Her gaze whipped back to his. "Excuse me?"

"That life you described doesn't protect you from heartache. I'm not Antwan. I'm not going to make promises I can't keep or say things I don't mean. Do I want to marry you? Hell, I don't know. I don't know if I ever really want to get married. Kids—I can't even imagine. Right now, all I want is you in my life. I don't know how we'd work out, and I can't promise you we will. But that doesn't mean I'm afraid to try. When you're ready to stop making excuses, come and get me."

He turned on his heels and walked away.

Chapter 18

I want you to be my girl.

Julie's stomach fluttered and her knees wobbled. She tried hiding both by smiling at the housekeeper who opened the door to let her into Dante's home.

Those words had floated around Julie's head since he'd uttered them the week before. Each time her heart celebrated, her brain slapped the silly organ into submission. She'd been someone's *girl* before. Played the role of ignoring whispers of infidelity, putting up with the phone calls and the groupies. She wouldn't do that again.

As she followed the housekeeper, Julie stiffened her resolve. She did want a future with a guy who wasn't a part of this life. She would be happy with a house in the suburbs, date nights on the couch and talks of what happened at the office. Dante wasn't into that.

Impromptu pool parties, concerts at his home on the weekend and wild parties in Vegas—that was his life.

She entered the spacious living area, and immediately her gaze searched for Dante. He stood across the room talking to his father. She'd recognize Otis Wilson anywhere. He was a superstar in his own right. Otis's blue suit was tailored perfectly to show off a body that nearly rivaled his son's despite the twenty-plus year difference in age. There were a few wisps of gray in his short, curly dark hair.

"Julie," Raymond said from her left.

Dante looked her way. Their gazes locked, and in that second, her heart skipped a beat. Tearing her gaze from Dante, she looked at Raymond. "Hey, Raymond."

"Guess who's coming tonight?" Excitement filled Raymond's voice.

"Who?" she asked, very aware that Dante and his father were crossing the room to them.

"The Roberson family."

Julie's eyes widened. "*The* Robersons?" Raymond nodded, and Julie's brain struggled to process the information. The Roberson family's legacy in music was almost as big as the Wilsons'. Julie loved their music and couldn't suppress her own wave of excitement.

Dante and his father made it to her side. "Julie," Dante said. "This is my father, Otis Wilson."

Julie smiled and held out her hand. Otis's dark gaze sized her up quickly, but she couldn't read his opinion after the quick examination.

"It's a pleasure to meet you, Mr. Wilson," Julie said. Holding back her starstruck grin was difficult.

"The pleasure is all mine, Ms. Dominick. Dante's

told me about the hard work you've put into opening our nightclub."

Julie glanced quickly at Dante, whose jaw hardened into a hard line. "I didn't realize you had an interest."

"I have an interest in every venture taken by my family. The Wilson name and legacy is the most important thing to me. I can't ignore anything that may hurt either."

His voice was smooth but underlined with steel. This nightclub was Dante's way to try his hand at building his own dream, his own legacy. She'd forgotten Dante said his father didn't support his plans. From the tone of Otis's voice, Julie guessed he had other ideas for the place. The thought disturbed her far more than it should.

"You know my wife and daughter, no doubt."

Otis turned to Vivica and Star, who had risen from the couch. They crossed the room looking like music royalty. Vivica's short, stylish hair was a deep russet color that complemented her light eyes and the deep red scooped-neck shirt she'd paired with black pants. Dante's sister, Star, wore a blue-and-white dress that clung to her curves while her jet-black hair hung to the middle of her back.

"Again, it's an honor to meet you both." She glanced to Star. "I've listened to your music and loved it for years."

Star gave a sincere smile and shook Julie's hand. "I'm glad you enjoyed it."

Otis turned to Julie. "What did you think of her last album?"

Star stiffened, and Otis watched Julie closely. Julie was well aware that her last album had been a flop that resulted in Star being ridiculed from those in and out of the industry.

"It was different," Julie said.

Otis smirked. "A nice way of saying the album was terrible. I told her not to do it."

"Actually, I liked the song on there about not being the guy's doormat," Julie said. "That was my favorite. I admire people who try something different. So many are afraid to leave the status quo."

"I appreciate that," Star said.

Vivica smiled at Julie. "How are things coming with the nightclub?"

"Very well. We had a few challenges but were able to get things back on track."

Raymond rubbed Julie's back. "Julie always handles her business."

Dante's eyes zeroed in on the movement, and Julie fought hard not to step away from Raymond.

"Does she now?" Otis said, his eyes also on the hand still at Julie's lower back. "How long have you two known each other?"

"Six or seven years," Raymond said. "Julie and I have been good friends since college."

"Raymond's like a brother to me." She looked to Dante but couldn't read much in his expression.

"And Julie's my heart," Raymond said.

Before she could reply, the rest of the guests arrived. Otis and Vivica were all bright smiles and hugs when the Robersons arrived. Julie's own lips spread with her excitement, which was short-lived when their daughter, Missy, came into the room. The five-foot-nine-inch pop singer was gorgeous: golden-brown skin, long blond hair and a body that was nothing but curves. A grown man's fantasy in a might-as-well-be-Velcro black dress that clung so good.

"Dante," Missy said in a throaty purr. Dante smiled and kissed the woman's cheek.

Julie's stomach soured. Dante and Missy had been music's most famous couple about four years ago. You couldn't turn on the television or open a magazine without seeing the two together.

Raymond moaned softly next to Julie. "She is so sexy."

Julie cut her eyes at Raymond. "And here I thought I was your heart."

Raymond grinned at Julie. "You had your chance to nab me the other day."

"How easily you move on," she said, teasing.

"You are my heart, Julie. Just because we agreed not to be in a relationship, it doesn't change the fact that I care about you. You're my oldest and closest female friend. You'll always be in my heart. No matter who you end up with."

"Raymond, sometimes I forget that beneath that playboy exterior of yours is the good guy who helped me mend my broken heart."

Raymond's devilish smile returned. "You're my girl, Julie. Remember that when I try to go home with Missy tonight."

Julie laughed and pushed Raymond's shoulder. When she glanced back, Dante was watching the two of them. His eyes were guarded. The welcoming smile he'd had when Missy came in was gone.

Dante cleared his throat and glanced away. "Now that everyone is here, we can eat."

Missy put her hand in Dante's. Julie wanted to slap Missy's hands out of Dante's.

"Looks like my chances are slim," Raymond said. "Not surprising. I overheard Otis telling Dante he should get back with Missy. He says it'll be good for business."

"Did he agree?"

"He didn't disagree," Raymond said.

Julie swallowed hard. Lifting her chin, she pushed away the hurt. This was for the best.

She zeroed in on Dante and Missy. Dante looked at her briefly, then turned to lead Missy into the dining area. *You pushed him away. Men like Dante don't sulk.*

"We should go," Julie said, dismissing the thought. Raymond nodded and put his hand on her lower back again to escort her to the dining room.

Jealousy seared through Dante's gut like battery acid, preventing him from enjoying the meal. He felt like he was in some crazy parallel universe. Julie on Raymond's arm, laughing with him like they were... well, old friends. Him, entertaining Missy after his dad mentioned, after the fact, that he'd invited the Robersons to dinner. In a heartbeat, he and Julie had gone from lovers to this distant business-friendly relationship.

"Dante," Otis said. "Despite the fight, I heard good things about the song you did at your party."

Dante snapped his mind out of the clouds and focused on his father. "I'll admit that even I was surprised at how much they liked my collaboration with S.A.F. I'm sure an album with them will be hot."

Otis scowled. "I'm not talking about that. I mean your collaboration with Antwan."

Missy ran her fingers over Dante's arm. "It's hot, Dante, just like you."

Dante gripped the fork in his hand. "I'm not going to do the album with Antwan."

Otis leaned back in his chair. "Yes, you are. We've already started promoting the upcoming collaboration. You need to do everything you can to keep the momentum going." He looked meaningfully between Dante and Missy.

Dante knew the meaning behind that look, and understood the reason the Robersons and Missy were at dinner. An album with Antwan combined with a reunion between Dante and Missy would mean the federal government couldn't print money fast enough to keep up with the sales.

Dante glanced at Julie, but she studied her food. He wondered if seeing him with Missy caused the same battery-acid corrosion of her insides that he felt when he thought of her with Raymond.

"I'm not interested in owning the charts. I'm ready to do my own thing, including the nightclub."

"Don't you care anything about our family's legacy?" Otis vented.

Dante looked back at his father. "You know that I do."

"Building and holding a legacy takes planning. You've got to lay the groundwork. One year—hell, six months without proving that you belong at the top is enough time to make others forget your contribution to the music industry."

Vivica leaned forward. "Your father is right, Dante. After your sister's last album, we need to do whatever it takes to remind people that the Wilson legacy is still strong."

Star flinched but didn't disagree. Dante hated to see how she just took her parents using her failed album as putting them on the cusp of ruin.

"People love a comeback," Dante said. "When Star puts out new music, then they'll love her, and no one will care about that one album."

Star smirked. "That's not true, Dante, and you know it. They'll move on, but they'll never forget. We need a big splash to remind people why W. M. Records is at the top. I agree with Dad—you should do the album with Antwan."

Dante looked to Missy. "What do you think?"

The smile on her beautiful face made most men lose their ability to speak. "I support you in everything you do, Dante." Her hand rubbed his arm, and she lowered her eyes prettily. "But I do agree with your family. I know your little project is important, and you can still dabble in that after doing the song with Antwan." She lifted her eyes and dropped her hand to his knee. "Then we can collaborate again. I miss working with you."

Her tone implied that she missed a lot more than a musical collaboration. Dante shifted until her hand fell away from his knee. He glanced again at Julie, but this time, she was studying the art on the wall. He'd think she didn't care if her jaw wasn't clenched so tight. Hope blossomed in his chest. She was jealous, and if she were jealous, that meant she had to care.

"That's nice, Missy, but I want someone who'll support me, my new music and my plans. Not just encourage me to do the same thing over and over."

Star grunted. "Dante, don't be crazy. You saw how the press obliterated me after this last album."

Dante turned to his sister. "That's because you were insincere. You were trying to be something you're not, and people saw that."

"Wouldn't you be doing the same with this album?"

Julie made a noise, and everyone looked her way. She glanced around the table, then met Dante's eyes. "No, he wouldn't. I've heard the music and seen him perform with S.A.F. Dante's really into this sound— you can hear it, feel his intensity with every note. It's not the same as his other music. It's more real. More him."

A swirl of emotion Dante was too unfamiliar with to name rose in his chest. That's why he wanted her.

Otis grunted. "That's a nice sentiment, Ms. Dominick, but sentiment isn't what sells music."

"I'd disagree," Julie said. "Music speaks to people. A song can make you laugh, cry, fall in love. Music is nothing but a mixture of various sentiments, and that's what makes you love an artist. If their music pulls at something deep inside of you, you never forget. When you hear the same emotions you're struggling with in one of their songs, it becomes your favorite."

Otis raised his chin and regarded Julie for several seconds. "I can't disagree with you on that."

"Then would you agree that if Dante does music with Antwan, even though he doesn't want to, people may notice the disconnection?"

Otis's eyes narrowed. "Well said, Ms. Dominick."

"Julie," she said, raising her chin.

Otis watched her for a second, then turned back to Dante. "Did I tell you that I saw Octavia Quinn in New

York last week?" Otis said, referring to another music producer.

Dante let his dad change the subject. For Otis to do so meant he needed to consider Julie's point. The argument with Otis wasn't over, but Julie had given him another weapon in the war. Dante glanced at her and gave her a thankful smile. Her quick argument had probably done more to make his case than anything he could have ever said to his own father. Otis loved his kids, but he also was used to running their lives, especially when it came to music.

Missy shifted at his side, and placed her hand on his knee again. Julie turned to talk to Raymond, and in that beat, the connection was gone.

Chapter 19

"I appreciate the way you stood up for my son in there," Otis said as they left the dining room and walked into the sitting room. He stopped her at the door. "You must really care about him."

"Caring has nothing to do with it. Like I said to Star, I admire those who are willing to go after their dreams."

Otis nodded. "I work with Nexon-Jones, and I know why you really left."

"What is it that you think you know?"

"That you brought up a complaint against the owner after he offered you a project if you were willing to sleep with the client."

"A project isn't worth my self-respect."

"Because of that, I don't believe the rumors that you're out here because there's something going on between you and Dante. I need you to remember that you are his business partner only. While I appreciate your willingness to step in and offer your support, at the end of the day, Dante always does what's right for the family. He'll make the album with Antwan, and he'll get back together with Missy. Both are good for business, despite any sentiments that may temporarily distract him."

The words had their desired effect. She was just a temporary person in Dante's life. Her small amount of support while she was out here would not change a lifetime of choices. People didn't change unless they wanted to, and Dante had given no real signs that he wanted to change his lifestyle. He just accused her of not being truthful about what she wanted.

"I'm very aware of that. I'm here to get the nightclub opened. Whatever happens after that is up to Dante."

She nodded at Otis and walked farther into the room. Dante watched her from where he stood with Missy. The beautiful singer talked, but he didn't appear to be listening. There was something different in his eyes as he watched her. Something she wanted to believe was an emotion deeper than lust. But she knew the rules. She'd stood up for him, and now he was grateful.

She was ready to go back to her hotel room and try not to think about how her unavailability left plenty of room for Missy to snuggle up in his bed. She walked over to Dante and Missy. "I'm going to leave now. Thank you for inviting me to dinner."

Dante frowned. "Are you sure?"

"Yes, it's been a long week, and I'm tired."

Raymond came over. "Julie, you're leaving. I can give you a ride back to your hotel."

Julie shook her head. "No need, I drove."

"Before you go, do you have a few minutes? I want to talk to you about the opening," Dante said.

She'd given him an update yesterday and was about to refuse when Missy shifted closer to Dante and stared at him with barely disguised lust. *Looks like Raymond's hopes are dashed.*

"Sure, let's talk," Julie said.

"We can talk in my office." He stepped away from Missy. "Just give us a few minutes."

"Hurry back," Missy said.

Julie followed Dante out of the sitting room and into his office down the hall, a room with gleaming modern furniture, a high-end computer and posters of his album covers on the wall, including the one with him in nothing but a pair of boxers. The album was titled *Sex*, and it was released when she was nineteen. She'd drooled over that picture too many times that year.

Julie didn't go far into the room and stood right inside the door. Dante pushed the door closed and leaned his hand against the wood. He watched her, his dark eyes swimming with what made her want to be his girl.

"What did you want to know?" She took a step backward.

"That was an excuse to get you in here. Thank you for what you said at dinner."

Julie shrugged. "I'm nothing if not honest."

"That you are. Even though you've been to the studio and listened to us play, I hadn't realized you felt that way about my music."

He leaned forward and stared at her.

"I love your music. The music you're making is

beautiful, vibrant and full of everything that makes you who you are."

"I put everything I have into my music." He crossed his arms and leaned on the door. "Sometimes I think about the arguments my dad makes. I don't want to do the same mainstream stuff everyone else is doing, but I don't know what to do if I fail."

"They are right. Your song with Antwan is hot, so you still have some spark for what you've been doing."

"That's because I love music. Early in my career, everything was new. I didn't care much as long as I got the next hit, owned the charts—" he met her eye "—landed the girls. Now it's not so much about that. I still care about my brand, but I've fallen in love with the actual creativity of my job again. Now that I've rediscovered my love of creating something, I don't know if I can give it up."

He sounded so conflicted, as if he had already accepted that he would have to give up his dream. As someone who understood how hard fighting for success could be, she reached out and cupped his face in her hands. Dante blinked and focused his dark eyes on her. "Then don't give up."

The smile he gave her was small, sad. "It's easier to believe I can do this when you're around. When you leave, it'll be the status quo again."

"You started this before I ever came into your life. You'll finish when I'm gone."

She pulled her hand back. His shot out to gently grab her wrist. He pulled her against him. Julie pressed her palm to his hard chest. The heavy beat of his heart tapped against her palm, every vibration resonating through her body.

"I meant what I said the other day. Don't talk about leaving as if it were nothing." His hand gripped her waist, holding her closer until the heat of his body seeped into her bones.

"I never said leaving you would be easy."

Dante shifted forward, his chest brushing the hardening tips of her breasts. His warm hand released her wrist to brush against her jaw. Julie's heart thudded, pumping blood through her in quick spurts.

"No rules, no games, just the truth. You don't like me saying I want you to be my girl, fine—I won't say that. But I do want you, Julie. You can argue all day about wanting some quiet life with some quiet guy who's squeaky-clean, but that won't satisfy you."

"How do you know that?"

"Because there is fire and fight in you. You'd eat a guy like that up, then spit him out in no time. You need a guy who isn't going to back down when you toe the line and won't let you use excuses to talk yourself out of going for what you want."

"Maybe so, but that doesn't mean you're the right guy."

"Maybe I'm not. I can't say for sure that I'm your forever guy, but I know one thing—if we don't try to make this work, we'll both regret it."

"You won't have time to regret it. Raymond overheard your dad saying he wants you and Missy back together. Otis repeated same thing to me."

"My dad said that to you?"

"Yes. See, you've already got your rebound set up. I'm moving aside with no drama. You're free to be with Missy."

She tried to step away, but his grip tightened on her

waist. He pulled her forward, his eyes flashing with desire. "I'm not begging Missy to be with me right now, am I? No games, no rules, just honesty. Tell me right now, Julie, that you don't want to give this a try."

She shook her head and looked away. "I don't want to—"

He cut her off with a kiss. The lie she was about to tell was forgotten, no longer important because his lips were on hers. No matter how hard she tried to control her cravings for this man the second their lips touched nothing else mattered. Her hands clenched his shirt and pulled him closer. His head tilted, and the soft sweep of his tongue against her lips was his sensual demand for more. Julie quickly parted her lips. Her arms lifted to wrap around his neck.

Only a kiss. That's all she was going for. His hand on her waist moved to grip her ass and pulled her farther into his body. No way could she walk out that door without more.

Dante's strong arm lifted her. Their bodies moved before he set her down on the top of the table next to the door. Vaguely, she thought about the room full of people next door, how easily they could get caught and why they should stop. Then his hands were on her breasts. His fingers rubbing and squeezing the heavy flesh, toying with her aching nipples. Julie jerked up his shirt and ran her hands over the hard planes of his stomach. Between slitted lids she watched him in the dim lights. She watched the play of his muscles beneath his shirt, the fire burning in his dark eyes and the urgency of his movements. He wanted her, and in that second, she wished for forever.

"Dante," she whispered his name.

His head rose, and he brushed his fingers through her short hair. "Julie." His voice was low, deep, possessive. Long fingers pushed her skirt up and slipped into the side of her panties.

Eyes rolling upward, Julie's head fell back, her legs widened. Pulling her head forward with the hand that was in her hair, Dante claimed her mouth with another searing kiss. Julie unbuttoned his pants, freeing him from his briefs. Her fingers wrapped around the hard length before slowly sidling down to gently cup the heavy sac beneath.

Stepping back only to push down his pants and pull out a condom, Dante slid on the protection, then came back to kiss her. One hand pushed her panties to the side. He positioned himself at her opening, then thrust forward.

"Mmm, Dante, yes," she moaned. Her leg wrapped around his waist.

He gripped her waist with one hand; the other cupped her face. He kissed her slowly, thoroughly, while his body pushed in and out. His entire body tensed, humming with the same pleasure that had Julie panting and moaning. He broke the kiss to suck on her neck. Inhaling deeply, he groaned. "Damn, Julie."

Hips pumping harder, Dante broke her walls. All the emotions she didn't want him to expose tumbled around inside her. She was screwed, so royally screwed for falling for a guy like him. A guy that made her want to try to make something work and trusted that they could. Her body shattered in waves of pleasure. Her leg squeezed him tighter, and her vision blurred.

Dante's rhythm slowed, then stopped. The world came back into focus. He lifted his head, the triumph in his eyes unmistakable. His hand squeezed her thigh. "Be my lady, Julie. Say you'll be mine."

Her body froze. The words were different, but the situation and the tone all the same—words asking for a forever that came right after sex. *Never trust what was said during sex*, another rule she followed. Words of love and promises of forever could always be blamed on throes of pleasure, and when brought up later, considered unfair. She'd say yes and think she and Dante could work, only to find him back to his old arrogant ways in no time.

She pushed Dante away and jumped off the table. When he reached for her, she pulled away.

"Julie, what's wrong?"

She kept her back to him while she fixed her skirt. "I've got to go." He reached for her again, but she opened the door and escaped.

Chapter 20

"I had sex with him, on a table, with his parents in the next room."

A heavy sigh came through Julie's cell phone after her confession. Julie pictured Evette cringing on the other end.

"You didn't?"

"I did, which is why I need to go ice queen and leave him alone. I don't think straight when I'm with him."

"Sometimes you don't want to think straight."

Julie snorted and stared out of her hotel window at the mountains in the distance. "Not thinking straight gets you in trouble."

"But sometimes it can lead to a lifetime of happiness."

Julie rolled her eyes because Evette wasn't there to see it. "Who do you know that's had a lifetime of happiness with a guy like Dante? First I was a challenge and didn't just fall into his bed. Now that I have, I'm an interesting conquest, but that's it."

Be my lady, Julie. Say you'll be mine.

Dante's words rang through her head. But words spoken after sex, on a table, with his family one wall over, were not words that made a strong foundation for a relationship.

"Can you, for once, stop analyzing everything a man does in a relationship and just go with things?" Evette asked.

"This has nothing to do with my rules." So what if not trusting words spoken during sex was one of her biggest rules?

"It has everything to do with them. You're probably reciting them in your head right now."

Damn Evette and her insightfulness. "Maybe I should recite them constantly. From the moment I got here, I've ignored my rules and got involved with Dante. I need to finish this project and get the hell out of California."

"Look, I can't say whether or not Dante is the right guy for you. He is a big party guy and is linked to a lot of different women, but—"

"How can you possibly have a but?"

"But," Evette said, enunciating the *t*, "knowing that you've gone against your normally rigid stance, I think you have some feelings going on for the guy. And," Evette said in a hurry, as if she could sense Julie opening her mouth to argue, "for him to ask you to try to make things work between you makes me believe there's more going on than raging libidos and a need for a conquest."

"Maybe, but that also doesn't mean the lifetime of

happiness you referred to. Before I lost my mind and slept with him on a table—"

"With his parents in the next room."

Julie groaned. "Before all that, he was laughing with his beautiful ex-girlfriend, who stuck to him better than pantyhose in the summer. His dad wants them back together to boost his career, and there's a good possibility he's going to be working with Antwan."

"Good possibility isn't definite fact. He screwed you on a table, not his beautiful ex-girlfriend. Points to Julie."

Julie thought about the intense pleasure from that incident and twisted her thighs together. "Who knows what he did after I left."

"If you would've stayed, he probably would've screwed you on another table, then the bed, maybe even the pool."

"Evette, stop!" Julie jumped up from the chair. Her mind and body going into sexual overdrive with all the possibilities. "None of that matters. He's just like Antwan, and I'm not going down that road again. He's not the guy for me."

"Then who is the quote-unquote guy for you, Julie?" Evette asked with exasperation.

"Huh?"

"Who's this dream guy you're waiting on? You are hit on by more men than anyone I know. Most women would love to have the guys you repeatedly shoot down ask them on a date. You keep saying you're waiting for someone outside of the business, but even when you meet a guy like that, you never trust him enough to let him get close. I'm not telling you to ride off into the sunset with Dante, but you need to take a long, hard look at yourself and what you really want. Because for someone who says they eventually want a relationship, you're too mistrusting to ever get there."

Evette's words stung. That was the way with the truth. Julie ran her hand over her face and sighed. "I just don't want to get hurt."

"I know. Antwan broke your heart. Raymond wanted to be the next guy, but he was too busy sleeping with anything with two X chromosomes. A lot of the men we meet are just trying to play games, but that's life. You and every other woman out there are dealing with the same thing. Eventually, you have to stop using not wanting to get hurt as an excuse to throw away a chance at love or just accept that you're old and bitter."

"I'm not bitter."

"I can get a thesaurus and look up another word for it, but the meaning's the same."

Julie wasn't ready to cave in just yet. "You heard about the fight—there are already rumors that I got this job because I'm sleeping with Dante. If I openly date him, then what? More proof that my big projects are because I'm involved with the men."

"It doesn't matter if you never sleep with a client, people will always make their own judgments. Next excuse?"

"Once this project is done, I'm back in Atlanta, and he's still here trying to decide if he should hook up with his ex."

"Okay, that's kind of a good one," Evette admitted. "But not good enough to not even try. There was a chance Dominant Development would fail, but you still gave it a try. Stop being afraid, and admit that you're really into Dante."

"Fine. I am." Julie stomped her foot. Frustration and fear bubbled in her stomach. "I can't let myself hope that he feels the same. I can't go with my feelings and get caught up in thinking that this will be a real relationship only to end up exactly where I was years ago, heartbroken, when he tells me I've become one of many. So, yes, there's more going on. Yes, I feel like I'm falling in love with him. Yes, I want to give this a try, but for my own self-preservation, I'm keeping my focus on opening this club and leaving without him ever knowing how I feel."

Julie sucked in several ragged breaths. Her heart pounded. Evette didn't immediately answer. Guess that was the way of things when someone, normally so put together, had an outburst over the telephone. A rush of words that proved just how scared Julie was.

"Oh, Julie." Evette's voice had the sympathetic and comforting tone of a mother about to give heartwarming advice to a forlorn teenager.

Julie didn't want to hear it. Evette hadn't been humiliated and broken the way Julie had when Antwan laughed at her in front of a club full of people.

"I've got to go. I'll call you tomorrow." Julie ended the call before Evette could finish.

Chapter 21

Dante burst into the studio. His mind still reeled over how easily Julie ran away the night before. He'd never, *ever*, put himself out there like that. He'd asked—no, practically begged for a woman to admit that she had feelings for him. That wasn't what Dante Wilson did. He was supposed to be in control of his own life, his own destiny. Now he was fluttering in the wind. He was caught up in a relationship Julie didn't want while simultaneously being forced to make an album he didn't want.

"What's wrong with you?" Terrance asked. He and Tommy stood next to the piano reviewing music.

"Too many people in my head trying to tell me what to do," Dante answered.

"The album with Antwan?" Tommy asked.

Dante nodded, not willing to admit the feelings he had for Julie also contributed to his foul mood.

"My dinner with my family last night was supposed to persuade them that opening this nightclub and doing my own thing to promote Strings A Flame and our music is what I should be doing next. Instead, they invite Missy, have already started promoting this new album and, based on the latest blog by our friend Gary—" Dante pulled out his cell and waved it "—Missy and her family having dinner at my house last night marks the beginning of us getting back together."

He slammed the cell on the top of the piano. Rubbing his eyes with the heels of his hands, Dante clenched his teeth to keep from yelling his frustration.

Terrance frowned and leaned one arm on the piano. "Wasn't Julie there? How did she take things?"

Dante dropped his hands and smirked at Terrance. "Remarkably calm. She basically told me to move on, and that I'm free to pursue whatever I want with Missy."

Right before making love to him and joining his heart with hers. Even if she didn't realize that.

"I don't believe that," Terrance said.

"You didn't see the impassive look in her eye when she said it." Or feel the pain in Dante's chest that resulted afterward.

"Julie was here in the studio cheering you on. I see the way she looks at you. That woman is crazy about you."

"Well, she's not crazy about being crazy about me. She doesn't want a relationship with me. She wants to go back to Atlanta, and find some guy outside of the music industry to settle down with. Some guy who won't have groupies throwing panties at him after a show or twin supermodels offering threesomes at parties."

Tommy chuckled. "That is your life."

"That was my life before Julie. It wouldn't be my life if I had Julie."

"Did you tell her that?" Terrance asked.

Dante looked at Terrance and shrugged. "I did, but she doesn't believe me. She won't say it, but I know she's comparing me to Antwan."

Tommy scowled. "Why?"

"Because they dated once, and he treated her like he treats most women." Dante's voice filled with disgust. Mostly for himself—he'd treated women the same. Beautiful conquests with little regard to what happened when he was ready to move on.

Tommy and Terrance flinched. "He may make good music," Tommy said. "But he's not the person I'd recommend as the example for what it's like to date a musician."

"Tommy's right, Dante," Terrance said. "You've got to show her that you're serious."

"How can I show her that when she's not even willing to give me the chance to prove myself?"

"By not giving up and doing something she wouldn't expect from a guy who was only interested in having a little fun."

Dante sat on the piano stool and ran a hand over his face. He thought about what he'd done the night before and chuckled.

"What?" Terrance asked.

"I wrote a song about her. I haven't done that in years—written a song about a particular woman. Last night, I couldn't get the feelings out of my head until finally I grabbed a notebook and started writing."

Tommy held out his hand. "Let us see."

"It's no good. Just some feelings running in my head. Nothing that needs to see the light of day."

Tommy didn't drop his hand. "Words written with feeling always deserve to see the light of day."

Terrance nodded. "He's right, Dante. Let us hear the lyrics."

Dante looked at the two brothers. Heat burned across his neck and cheeks. They'd think he was crazy or that he was crazy in love. He never should have said anything about writing the music. Damn sure shouldn't have spent the night writing a song about a woman who'd turned him down more than any other woman he'd ever met.

He glared at Tommy's outstretched hand, then met his expectant look. They were musicians; they wouldn't laugh. Hopefully.

Sighing heavily, Dante pulled out the notebook in his backpack and slapped bound pages into Tommy's hand. Terrance scooted next to his brother and took a look. For several tense seconds, Dante watched as they read over the words that had thrummed through his mind the night before.

"Have you thought of the beat to go with it?" Terrance asked.

"Not quite. I'm hearing something, but it's not coming clear," Dante answered.

"Tell us what you're thinking—let's see what we can do."

Dante raised a brow. "Are you sure? This really isn't for production."

Terrance slapped the back of Dante's head. "Play the damn beat."

Dante rubbed the back of his head and glared at Terrance, who didn't look the least bit regretful.

"Fine," Dante gritted out. He swung around on the piano stool. Running his fingers along the cool keys, he took a deep breath, then strummed out the start of a melody that hovered at the back of his mind.

Terrance nodded, listening to the music. He picked up his violin and began to play, adding to Dante's piano melody. Tommy headed to the drums instead of picking up his own violin. He tapped out a beat, and instantly Dante could hear the song coming together.

For the next hour, they worked on the song. When the rest of the group came in, Dante gave them the pieces of the melody they'd worked out and continued to practice. By the end of the set, the words that hovered in Dante's mind were transferred from the notebook to the pages of several sheets of music. A rough draft, to say the least, but very close to being the finished product.

His cell phone rang after they ran through the song again. It was Otis. "Hold up, guys, I need to take this call."

He answered the phone on his way out and to the office next door.

"I'm calling to see if you're available for dinner with the Robersons again tonight. I think it'll be good to get reservations at Arata where you and Missy can be seen together."

Dante gritted his teeth to keep from cursing Otis out. "No. I'm not going to Arata with the Robersons. I'm not doing the same old songs I've always done, and I damn sure am not getting back together with Missy."

"Are you raising your voice at me?"

"Depends, are you trying to run my life?"

"No one is trying to run your life."

"Then stop thinking that the work I'm doing with S.A.F. is some little project. Stop stomping on my dream to do something different. Stop stepping to the woman I'm trying to be with and telling her that I belong with someone else. I'm a grown man. I'm not the thirteen-year-old who first started in this business. When I want your advice, I'll ask for it."

There was a long pause. "You're too big for my input now, huh?"

"I'll always value your opinion when I ask for it."

"You don't care about W. M. Records? Getting with Missy and the collaboration with Antwan are all a part of the plan to help revive sales." Otis's voice seethed with frustration and disbelief.

Dante did care. How could he not care for the company that was so much a part of his success? He also cared for his dreams. He couldn't let those go.

"*If* Antwan signs I'll consider a collaboration for his album. That's it."

"Will your mom and I at least see you for breakfast before we leave town tomorrow?" The anger had drained from Otis's voice.

"Yes."

"Good." Otis sighed. "I hope I didn't ruin things with Ms. Dominick."

"Nothing I can't fix." He hoped at least.

They ended the call. Dante felt as if a huge weight was lifted from him as he entered the studio again. Otis didn't say it, but Dante had won the battle.

The guys were all settled around the room. Tommy played the music they'd put together on his violin.

Esha and Terrance were on the sofa. Their arms were entwined, and they looked as if there was nowhere else in the world they'd rather be. Longing hit Dante hard. That's what he wanted with Julie. For her to be wrapped in his arms, smiling, happy, content in their relationship.

Tommy stopped playing and looked at Dante. "All good?"

Dante nodded. "All good."

"Alright. Now, what are you going to do with this?" He held up the pages that held the lyrics.

"I'm going to release it," Dante said.

Terrance's head tilted to the side. "You want to get your family's company to release it?"

Dante shook his head. "No. I'm going to release it. Or better yet, S.A.F. will. Independently, without giving my dad or the rest of the suits at his company the opportunity to strip the song of what it truly is. Then we'll put out the rest of our music. Just in time for the opening of the club."

Terrance and the rest of the group brightened with excitement. Exhilaration rushed through Dante's veins. He would step out on his own and pray to God he didn't fall on his face. This was what he really wanted to do. This song, this music, was just as hot as anything else he'd done. He had enough of a fan base to know they'd love it. He hadn't been in the music business for seventeen years and learned nothing.

The only way to convince Otis of that was to do it on his own. If Otis came to Dante later and asked for him and S.A.F. to produce their music for the company, he'd leave that to the group to consider. Though he'd much prefer to keep doing their music on their own.

Dante had more than enough clout in the music industry to get his music promoted without the machine behind his father.

"Dante, are you sure we can do this?" Terrance asked. "The club opens in a few weeks. That means we need all of our music ready."

"Our music is ready. I've been delaying putting it out because I've let my dad's offer linger in my mind too long." Terrance nodded, and Dante knew that even though they supported his decision either way, his hesitation was holding them back. "Let's show people what Strings A Flame is about."

Chapter 22

Julie looked around the finished space of the club and smiled. Dark wood and leather furniture, muted gold accents. Across from the stage was a two-sided bar that would serve patrons inside and those sitting outside overlooking the ocean. The place had a warm, welcoming feel. She turned to smile at the building inspector. "Are we good for the CO?"

The inspector wrote something on his inspection form before looking up to meet Julie's eye. None of the same doubt or resentment he'd harbored after the fiasco with the sprinklers was there. Julie knew he'd never admit it, but she'd impressed him with her efforts to turn this project around.

"I'll have the certificate of occupancy ready for you this afternoon. You can open up this weekend with no problems."

Julie's smile broadened, and she held out her hand to shake his. "I'll be there to pick it up before five."

He shook her hand and gave her a hesitant smile before walking out. Julie did a quick spin on her toes before stopping and grinning. She'd done it. She'd opened a nightclub with one of the music industry's biggest stars, in a city she'd never worked in before, only a week behind schedule and slightly above budget. The sprinkler thing had ended up costing them more, but thankfully Dante and Ray hadn't balked at the excess cost. She was just glad that was the only snafu of the entire process.

The opening party for the club the next evening was already one of the most anticipated events in the city. Julie planned to attend. As the developer, she wouldn't dare not be there to see the fruits of her efforts in full effect. She wouldn't stay long. She doubted Dante would even notice if she came or left. After she'd pushed him away, their relationship had been distant. Not that she blamed him. No man she knew would chase after a woman who'd pushed him away the second after they had sex. She'd made her position clear, and he'd respected it. She should be overjoyed, not nearly heartbroken by the thought.

She left the finishing touches to the workers in the nightclub and went back to her hotel. On the ride to the hotel, she called Dante to tell him they were good for tomorrow, but her call went unanswered.

"Dante, it's Julie. I want you to know that I'll pick up the CO for the building this afternoon. Everything is set for the opening tomorrow. If you have any questions, give me a call. I'll be at my hotel."

Her voice was cool, formal. None of the inner turmoil she felt after turning him away showed through. Her biggest rule—never show the other party your hand. Right now, her hand was full of broken hearts. She never should have crossed the line. Now she was in love with a man she couldn't be with. Not truly.

After she ended the call, the commercial on the radio ended, and the announcer spoke.

"And we're back with Dante Wilson here in the studio. Dante tell us about this new nightclub you're opening."

Julie's foot nearly slipped on the gas. She sat forward and twisted the volume knob up until Dante's voice filled the car.

"It's not your typical spot," Dante said. "I want to showcase my music there."

"Your music? Haven't we heard your music for nearly twenty years?"

"You've heard a version of my music, but this is the music that I really want to do. It's a fusion of hip-hop, rhythm and blues, jazz and classical. Throw in some lyrics that speak to what I'm feeling, and you've got a new sound."

"A new sound. After what happened with your sister last year, I'm surprised you're venturing into new territory."

"I'm not here to talk about Star or what she did. I'm only here to promote my music. You've got to do what's in your heart. For most of my career, I did that, but working on this new album with this group has given me a new sense of purpose in my music. The club will showcase them and other artists in the future. For those who don't want to just follow the crowd and are willing to find their own flow, my spot is the place to be."

Julie grinned, knowing that his words were a challenge. No one liked to consider themselves part of the status quo. By promising something different, he would pique the interest of everyone in the vicinity.

"All right, then let's hear some of this new music. Tell me about this song I'm about to play."

"It's something new. Something that was rolling around in my head, and I had to get the words out. I think anyone who's ever fallen in love unexpectedly will relate."

"What do you know about unexpected love?" The announcer's voice dripped with curiosity.

"I know that just when you think things are going great as they are, the perfect person can walk into your life and show you all the things you never knew you wanted. The song is called 'Turned Tables' because I had a woman do that to me. I didn't want or expect to fall, but I did."

"Can I ask who?"

Dante chuckled, and tingles spread across Julie's body. "You can ask, but I won't tell."

The announcer laughed. "Fine, but you know now everyone is going to be anxious to find out who turned the tables on you. You heard it here first. Dante Wilson has fallen in love, and this song is for that lucky woman who landed this sexy man."

Julie's heart and mind raced. She barely heard the first bars of the music or the words to the song. He'd fallen in love? With who? Her? Julie shook her head. That was crazy. They'd barely spoken the past few weeks. He couldn't mean her. He'd never said anything about love. She'd made sure to hide any indication that her feelings were going in that direction.

Don't be silly, Julie. Of course he's not talking about you.

She shook her head again. For once, she didn't want to listen to the voice of reason in her head, to the voice that said to never hope. The voice that was turning her into the bitter woman Evette accused her of being.

Getting out of her head, Julie listened to the words of the song, hoping to get an idea of who he could be talking about.

*You turned the tables on me
Snatched my heart and threw it away
You turned the tables on me
Grabbed my love and said no way*

*I never wanted love
Never wanted to be that guy
But you came into my life
Snuck into my mind
Then turned the tables and snatched my heart
away*

Julie's heart pounded; her palms sweated. His voice oozed with love and pain. Had she hurt him? No, ending things was for the best. He was considering his dad's deal and would be working with Antwan if he accepted. He had Missy and twin supermodels to fall back on. But this guy, the guy singing, didn't sound like someone waiting on supermodel twins or superstar ex-girlfriends to fill the void.

Without realizing it, Julie had driven to her hotel. The valet attendant watched her through the driver's window, a friendly smile on his face. He probably thought she was crazy. Maybe she was for wanting the song to be about her. Julie got out of the car and handed over the keys. She stood outside in the sunshine, thinking. For the first time in a long time, she felt like her logic concerning relationships may be flawed.

Chapter 23

Julie entered the nightclub at ten the next night. Outside a line trailed past the door with people waiting to get in. Inside people crowded the bar and filled every table. The dim lights reflected off the dark wood and leather furniture. The second floor was reserved for VIPs, and with the best views of the stage, it was crowded with other musicians and celebrities.

Julie wanted to squeal with delight. This had to be the best club she'd opened yet. Thanks to the partnership with Dante and Raymond, she was sure it would be around for years to come. Maybe she and Dante would be together just as long. She wasn't going to push him away anymore. Not if he wrote the song for her.

And if he still wants you. Her stomach fluttered. That was a big *if.*

"Julie." Esha's voice came from the crowd.

Pushing away the doubt, Julie scanned the crowd until she spotted Esha at the bar. Julie wove through the crowd to her side.

"Don't get up," Julie said before Esha could stand. She leaned in to hug her. "Opening night is a hit, huh?"

"To say the least. This is fantastic. But I'm still nervous."

"About the performance?"

Esha's head bobbed up and down, her bright eyes wide. "Yes. Everyone seems to be okay with the music, but the performance will really show what's up."

Julie recognized that the music playing in the background was the fusion sound similar to what S.A.F. played. The bobbing heads and swaying bodies meant so far no one hated the music.

"Don't worry," Julie said. "S.A.F. makes great music. I know people will love it."

"You're just saying that because you need your new nightclub to be a hit."

Julie laughed. "True, but I also want S.A.F. to be successful. I love the music. It deserves to be heard by many."

Esha leaned back against the bar and grinned. "I see why Dante likes you so much. You really do care about what he's doing."

The nervous fluttering in Julie's stomach increased in rhythm. She hadn't called Dante after hearing his song on the radio. Fear of rejection was hard to overcome, and she didn't want him to laugh at her over the phone. Not that getting laughed at in person was any better, but at least face-to-face she could gauge his reaction when he saw her. Would there be elation, desire, the same hope dancing in her, or indifference, disgust, anger? His reaction would set the tone for how she proceeded.

"I am into what he's doing. I just wonder if he's into me as much as I'm into him." Saying the words out loud was kind of freeing.

"You heard the song. I know he is."

"We don't know the song is for me."

"Who else could it be about?"

Missy! the ever-pessimistic voice of reason shouted in her head. She would be optimistic about this. She wanted Dante. She had no clue how or if they could make a relationship work, but if he'd written the song about his feelings for her, she was willing to try.

"Have you seen him?"

Esha shook her head. "Not since earlier. They're about to start the show, so I'm not sure. We can check backstage."

Esha stood, and Julie followed her through the crowd to the back, where they flashed their backstage passes to the security guards. Julie's stomach twisted and fluttered the entire time. She was going to go with her instinct and trust her feelings for Dante. She only hoped she was right for going against all the rules that guarded her heart.

They found Dante and the rest of S.A.F. backstage. Julie's gaze landed on Dante, and she couldn't breathe. Missy stood before him, her arms wrapped around his shoulders. His hands were on her waist. Julie's heart, her hope, shattered into a million jagged pieces. What kind of a fool was she for thinking he'd written a song about her?

Maybe she made a sound. Maybe he felt the sharpness of her gaze. Maybe he just needed a break from staring at the dazzle that was Missy, but Dante looked directly at her. He didn't scramble to pull away from Missy. Instead he slowly slid his arms from around her waist and lowered his head to say something to her. Missy glanced over her shoulder at Julie; she cocked a brow before nodding and stepping aside.

Dante crossed the room to her. Even when her hope for them was broken, she couldn't deny he was devastatingly handsome with a dark shirt, fashionably worn jeans, maroon jacket and platinum chain. He took her breath away, made her body heat with remembrance.

He stopped in front of her. His dark gaze slid over her from head to toe. "You came." He sounded normal, not excited, nervous or even happy.

"Of course I came. I always come to the opening of my new nightclubs."

His head tilted. "Is that the only reason you're here?"

"What other reason do I have to be here?" Admitting the reason she really came now, after seeing him and Missy so close, made her cheeks burn.

His jaw clenched, and he ran a hand over his chin. "I'd hoped..." He trailed off.

"You and Missy look comfortable."

"Missy came to congratulate me and wish me well. She hugged me."

"It looked like a lot more than a hug." God, did she have to sound so jealous? She cleared her throat, looked away and then crossed her arms.

"It wasn't anything more than that. Why do you always have to try to find the bad in things?" He sounded disgusted.

Her heart hurt even more. Her defenses went up. "Because it's hard to trust the good you want to see."

"Do you really want to see the good?"

Before she could answer, Terrance came over. "Dante, it's time to start the show."

Dante frowned but nodded. He turned back to Julie. "We'll finish this conversation later."

He watched her for several more seconds before turning to join Terrance. Julie went back out to join the rest of the crowd. Surrounded by people, she felt alone and silly. She pulled out her phone and texted Raymond. He should be here.

Almost there.

He texted back. Relief swept through her. At least if he was there, he would distract her for a while before he found someone to go home with.

Dante and S.A.F. came onto the stage, and the crowd cheered. Dante grabbed the microphone. "Are you ready to hear my music?"

A series of cheers and "yeahs" vibrated through the air.

"All right, let's do this." He turned to the group. "This is Strings A Flame, also known as S.A.F., and we're ready to show you what we can do."

Dante sat at the piano. The melody was slow, sensual notes hovering in the air. Then came Terrance and Tommy with their violins, and, finally, the drums and the turntables adding the hip-hop flare. The crowd got into the music—clapping, cheering and dancing. Song after song, the ones with Dante on vocals and the ones without, were all received by the crowd with growing enthusiasm.

Julie was so proud to see that the place she'd helped

develop had such a fantastic start and how much the crowd responded to Dante's music. No matter what, she knew there would be a place for him in the industry. They went into one of their more upbeat dance numbers. Julie temporarily forgot her shattered dreams as she smiled and danced with the crowd. Then Missy jumped onstage and proceeded to twist and gyrate against Dante, which drove the crowd into further hysterics. Camera phones came out and people cheered them on.

The pain and humiliation from before slapped Julie's midsection. She spun away from the stage. The song ended. The clapping and cheering grew louder. Glancing over her shoulder, she caught Missy onstage, planting a kiss on Dante's lips. The pain in Julie's chest wouldn't have been worse if the crowd had danced on her heart. Squeezing her eyes shut, she swiveled and hurried to the exit. She was just at the door when the notes of the song she'd heard the other day started.

"This last song is dedicated to the woman who stole my heart," Dante said.

Julie froze, her hand on the door.

"One guess who that is." Missy's voice rang through the club.

The crowd cheered. No, the pain could get worse. Without looking back, Julie pushed out into the warm night.

Chapter 24

Dante snatched the microphone from Missy, but it was already too late. Julie was out the door. He glanced at Missy, at the excited crowd chanting for him to sing. His hand squeezed the microphone.

She'd turned him down, several times. She overanalyzed things. She'd automatically assumed the worst earlier. He should let her go. His chest tightened.

Turning, he made eye contact with Terrance and Tommy. They both smiled and nodded toward the door. Dante dropped the microphone and jumped off the stage.

He pushed through the crowd, ignoring the questions and sending up a quick prayer that bailing out on his first performance here didn't completely ruin his nightclub.

"I think Dante's going for the girl he really wants." Terrance's voice rang through the microphone.

Dante glanced back at his friend onstage and gave him the thumbs-up.

"Go get her," Terrance said.

Dante turned and ran from the club. He hoped to catch Julie. She couldn't have gotten her car from valet that quickly.

Outside he was greeted by a flash of cameras that temporarily blinded him. Dante held up his hands and glanced around. Raymond stood next to his Ferrari at the front of the valet line, frowning toward the driver's seat where Julie sat. She slammed the door closed. Raymond sighed and shook his head. A second later, the car jerked away from the curb. *Julie!*

Dante ran toward Raymond. "Julie, stop!" he yelled toward Julie's direction.

Raymond turned toward him as his car kept going. "What are you doing out here?"

Dante pointed toward the retreating vehicle. "Trying to catch Julie."

"She doesn't want to be caught. She said you and Missy were back together."

"I'm not with Missy. I'm not thinking about Missy. Didn't she know that damn song was about her?"

Raymond frowned. "It is?"

"Yes, and despite her efforts to keep pushing me away, I saw the look on her face before she ran out. She's just as crazy about me as I am about her. I want to be with her."

Raymond took a deep breath. "She's going back to her hotel. Have the valet bring your car round and go get her."

Dante briefly considered Raymond's change of heart, but he honestly didn't have time to really get into that.

He turned to the valets, knowing that no matter how fast they moved, the time would pass slowly.

"Just treat her right, Dante," Raymond said.

Dante turned and looked at Raymond as if he'd lost his mind. "Of course I'll treat her right. I love her."

The surprise on Raymond's face was comical. The feeling of admitting his feelings for Julie was exhilarating. He loved Julie.

A white BMW pulled up. Dante grinned and ran to the driver's side. After wrenching the door open, he practically jerked his sister out.

"Hey, Dante, what's going on?" Star squealed, scowling at him.

"No time, I need your car. Mine's in valet." He jumped in and put the car in gear. Ignoring the flash of the cameras, stunned looks and Star's screams for an explanation, Dante tore away from the curb.

Julie parked in front of the hotel. A young valet attendant strolled to her door, but she made no move to get out. Her entire body felt numb, startled into shock with the realization that she'd once again been humiliated and heartbroken by a guy at the opening night of one of her clubs. What else should she have expected? Of course he would move on after she pushed him away.

The attendant bent over to peer into her window. She couldn't sit there forever. Smiling weakly, she opened the door. He mumbled something about the night being good, and she wanted to tell the kid to get lost. She just wanted to go in, pack and go home. The club was open, and her part was done. Evette could handle the follow-up. Julie couldn't bear to talk to Dante again.

Tires squealed behind her. Julie spun just as a white BMW swung into the hotel parking area and jumped onto the curb in a haphazard park. Julie hopped back even though the car was far from hitting her.

"What the hell is wrong with you?" she yelled. She was ready to lash out at someone, and the crazy driver seemed like the perfect person.

The door opened, and Dante jumped out. Julie gasped, the hand over her racing heart fell to her side. "Dante?" Her voice was filled with all the longing that she'd denied herself. "What are you doing here?"

He stomped over to her. "Why did you run away?"

She frowned and shook her head. "What?"

"Why did you run away?" He towered above her, snatching her breath away and infusing her with the heat of his body. "If you don't care about me. If you really want me to do whatever I choose, and you don't want to give us a chance, then why did you run out of the club tonight?"

"Because…you and Missy. She said the song was for her."

"Don't be crazy, Julie. The song isn't about her."

"It's not?"

He shook his head. "Julie, who else would the song be about but you? I was happily single. I was enjoying my life, thinking I'd never *ever* want to be with just one woman. Now I'm completely uninterested in another chance with Missy and can't think of anyone but you. I need to know if what you told Raymond is true. That you really don't feel anything for me and this thing between us was just a hookup. Because if that's the case, I'll turn around and go back to the concert."

He pointed in the direction he'd come. "It'll hurt like hell, but I'll find a way to forget you."

Julie shook her head. "No. I don't want you to forget me." The words were out before she'd thought about them.

He didn't smile, just took a deep breath and stared at her with dark, wary eyes. "Then what do you want?"

Go hard or go home. She couldn't deny her feelings anymore. "I want you. Even though I know we may not be able to make this work."

The tension left his body, and warm hands lifted to cup her face. "We'll figure things out."

"I don't want you to feel like you're in a relationship that you can't really commit to."

"I can and I want to commit to you. I love you, Julie."

Joy, warmth and desire filled her heart. She smiled so hard her cheeks hurt. "I love you, too." No negative voice of reason made her feel crazy for admitting her feelings.

Dante pulled her into his arms. His firm lips pressed against hers, and she opened her mouth so he could deepen the kiss. The weight of years of fear from the results of trusting her heart with a man lifted from her shoulders. She wanted Dante, no games, no rules. The only rule that mattered was the one that said she was doing the right thing.

Chapter 25

Julie lounged on one of the chairs next to Dante's infinity pool, soaking up sun and drinking a margarita with Esha. Dante was having another one of the pool parties he was able to throw together within thirty minutes. Something that still boggled Julie's mind.

"Do you think he's really coming?" Esha said, grinning behind her glass.

Julie nodded. "In the ten months that I've dated Dante, he hasn't disappointed me yet. I believe him when he says he's coming."

Esha shifted on the chair. "I know that Dante knows him but to actually meet the guy in person…" Esha placed the frosted glass against her forehead. "I might faint."

Julie chuckled. "Better not let Terrance see that."

"Terrance knows that Irvin Freeman is my weakness. I would throw myself at him like a horny teenager if I didn't love Terrance, and if Irvin wasn't in love with that nurse he met."

"Well, good thing you love Terrance."

"You're awfully calm. Aren't you the least bit interested in throwing yourself at him?"

"No. I'm not." She sipped her margarita.

Julie was excited to meet the movie star, Irvin Freeman. The guy was one of Hollywood's biggest leading men—the fantasy of women everywhere, even more so now since he'd met a small-town nurse during a promotional weekend the year before, fallen in love with her and given up his career in front of the camera to be with her. Or so the stories went. Excitement wasn't enough to make her want to look at any guy other than Dante.

"Oh, my God," Esha exclaimed and gripped Julie's arm. "There they are."

Julie looked in the direction Esha stared at. Dante walked out onto the patio with a tall, handsome guy and a cute woman with an open smile. Julie instantly recognized them from the newspaper articles. Hollywood's current *it* couple were garnering a lot of attention from the other people at the party, but Julie only had eyes for Dante. His chest bare, a pair of red shorts sitting low on his hips and the sun shining down on all his sculpted perfection sent heat to her midsection.

She never would have thought she'd be so happy. When he'd asked her to stay on the West Coast after the club opened, she'd agreed. Surprisingly, Evette had encouraged her, even though Julie worried her friend would feel neglected. Julie was already working on another nightclub in LA while Evette oversaw redeeming Dominant Development's name by opening a new place in Miami. They were a two-office operation now. Julie could barely believe it herself.

Dante strolled over with Irvin and his girlfriend, Faith. Esha gushed, and Julie did her own blushing. Irvin didn't tempt her away from Dante, but she had to admit his smile up close was something to behold.

"Told you I know him," Dante said after Irvin and Faith left to change into their bathing suits. He'd promised to introduce her to the movie star after Julie got excited when Irvin earned a nomination for best director.

They sat on the edge of the pool with their feet in the water. Raymond played water polo with the rest of S.A.F.

"Yes, you did. So what do I owe you again?" she asked.

"Hmm, I'll have to think up something that involves you with a minimal amount of clothes."

Julie laughed and leaned into his side. "I don't consider that losing."

He wrapped an arm around her and pulled her in for a kiss. "Neither do I." He sighed and stared at the group in the pool. "So I got a call from my dad today."

"Really? What's up?"

"He wants to sign S.A.F. to the label. The success of the nightclub proved to him that I knew what I was talking about."

"That's great, Dante."

He shrugged. "We're not taking the deal."

Her eyes widened. "You're not?"

"No. I put the offer to the rest of the group, and they all decided we want to remain independent."

"How did your dad take the news?"

"I haven't told him yet. I'm good with the decision.

I'll still make music for the label and do a few collaborations like the one I did after they signed Antwan. I can't let W.M. go completely. It's my family legacy, but I want to keep this part of my music separate. I'm happy with the choice."

"I'm proud of you."

He grinned, then kissed her temple. "I heard more good news today, too."

Julie sipped from her glass and laughed when Raymond was hit in the head by the volleyball. "What else?"

"Irvin let it slip that he's going to propose to Faith. I think at the award show later this year."

Julie's eyes widened; her attention swung back to Dante. "That's fantastic. They are such a fairy-tale ending."

"Yeah, I can see that, but it kinda got me thinking that I want us to have our own fairy-tale ending."

"Oh, really?" she asked with a raised brow.

He reached into the pocket of his shorts. "Really." He pulled out his hand and held it up for Julie. A brilliant diamond ring sparkled on his pinkie.

Julie couldn't breathe. Her eyes jerked from the ring to his face. "Are you serious?"

"Yes. I know this is soon, but I also know what I feel. I love you, Julie. I've spent the past seventeen years chasing tail and having meaningless relationships."

"So not the time for that reminder."

"What I mean is, I know what's out there, and I don't want what's out there. I want you. Forever. We'll split our time between here and Atlanta. We'll make things work. I'd just rather make things work with my wife. Not my girl or my lady. Will you marry me?"

No voice of doubt. No pessimism. Just joy and the thought of spending her life with the man she loved. "Yes!"

He kissed her, pulled back to put the ring on her finger, then kissed her again. "I'm going to love you for the rest of my life, Julie. That's one rule I'll never break."

* * * * *

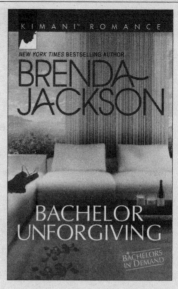

REQUEST YOUR FREE BOOKS!

2 FREE NOVELS
PLUS 2 FREE GIFTS!

KIMANI ™
ROMANCE

Love's ultimate destination!

SPECIAL EXCERPT FROM

*In med school, Felicia Blake couldn't help being
impressed by Griffin Kaile's physique, as well as his
intellect. The youngest of the accomplished Blake
triplets, Felicia put aside dating to focus on her
career. She may have fantasized about Griffin, but not
about discovering that he's the biological father of
the baby girl she's been asked to raise. Felicia is the
most stunning woman Griffin has ever known. Now
that the daughter he never knew about has brought
them together, he's eager to explore their romantic
potential. But ambitious Felicia is reluctant to jump
from passion to instant family. Which leaves Griffin
only one choice—to somehow show her that this kind of
breathtaking chemistry occurs only once in a lifetime...*

*Read on for a sneak peek at
TEMPTING THE HEIRESS, the next exciting
installment in author Martha Kennerson's
THE BLAKE SISTERS series!*

"Dr. Griffin Kaile," Felicia said, pulling herself together.
"It's been a while."

"Yes, it has, and you haven't changed a bit. You look
amazing," he said, smiling.

Felicia looked down at her outfit and frowned. "Not
really, but thanks. You look...professional."

Griffin smirked. "Thanks."

Professional. Really, Felicia? "How have you been?" she asked, breaking eye contact when she spied the gift from her sisters—red Valextra Avietta luggage—making its way down the carousel's runway. Felicia reached for the large wheeled trolley.

"I got it," Griffin said, placing his hand over hers.

Griffin's touch sent a charge through her body that she'd only felt one other time before, delivered by the same man. Felicia quickly pulled her hand from his and took a step back. "I'm doing well." Griffin picked up the large bag and placed it next to Felicia before reaching for his own leather suitcase.

"What a gentleman," Felicia heard a woman say.

"Thanks," Felicia said, smiling up at him.

"Last I heard, you were working somewhere overseas," Griffin said.

Felicia nodded. "I've spent the past year working in Asia."

"Wow, I bet that was an adventure. Are you in town long? We should get together…catch up," Griffin suggested, the corner of his mouth rising slowly.

"I…I'd really like that, but I'm only in town for the day. Unexpected and urgent business I have to tend to."

"I can't convince you to extend your trip?" Griffin asked, offering her a wide smile.

*Don't miss TEMPTING THE HEIRESS
by Martha Kennerson, available September 2016
wherever Harlequin® Kimani Romance™
books and ebooks are sold!*